"Megan doesn't remember her father."

"What kind of man was he, Kendra?" Brodie quirked a questioning eyebrow.

She rose to her feet. "You're out of line, Brodie."

"What's the big secret, Kendra? Why won't you talk about him? What are you hiding? Tell me *something* about your husband...or I'll start to believe you never had one!"

Her face turned whiter than a snowdrop petal. And her eyes filled with dismay.

"Dear God." Shock had him reeling. It had all been a lie—she'd been living a lie! But why?

Grace Green was born in Scotland and is a former teacher. In 1967 she and her marine-engineer husband, John, emigrated to Canada, where they raised their four children. Empty-nesters now, they are happily settled in west Vancouver in a house overlooking the ocean. Grace enjoys walking the sea wall, gardening, getting together with other writers...and watching her characters come to life, because she knows that, once they do, they will take over and write her stories for her.

Books by Grace Green

HARLEQUIN ROMANCE®

3526—THE WEDDING PROMISE
3542—BRANNIGAN'S BABY

His Unexpected Family

Grace Green

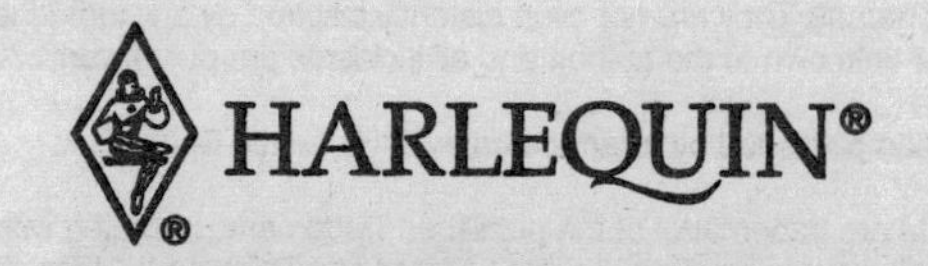

TORONTO • NEW YORK • LONDON
AMSTERDAM • PARIS • SYDNEY • HAMBURG
STOCKHOLM • ATHENS • TOKYO • MILAN • MADRID
PRAGUE • WARSAW • BUDAPEST • AUCKLAND

FOR MY NIECE CAROLYN

ISBN 0-373-17432-2

HIS UNEXPECTED FAMILY

First North American Publication 1999.

This edition published by arrangement with Harlequin Books S.A.

Look us up on-line at: http://www.romance.net

Printed in U.S.A.

CHAPTER ONE

"MOM, I want to go in by myself." Megan Westmore's dark eyes sparked with frustration. "I'll be eight next month, for heaven's sake—I'm not a *baby*!"

"But Lakeview Elementary's a new school for you and you're four days late starting the term—"

"Mom. I can *handle* it." Megan pushed open the door of the white Honda and scrambled out. "We talked with my homeroom teacher Friday. I know where to go. OK?"

Kendra Westmore looked at her daughter and marvelled, as she so often did, that she could actually be the mother of this child. Oh, they looked alike—they both had wheat-blonde hair and nut-brown eyes; fine bones and a petite build—but their personalities were poles apart. Megan was self-confident and fearless, while she, Kendra, was—

"'Bye, Mom." Megan hitched her backpack over her skinny shoulders. "See you at three-thirty." She slammed the car door and took off into the playground.

Without once looking back.

Kendra sighed. She knew she was overprotective of her daughter but she couldn't seem to break herself of the habit. Megan was all she had in the world. She didn't know what she'd do if anything ever happened to her—

The clangor of the school bell made her jump.

Reluctantly, she put the car into drive.

But as she moved forward a red pickup truck screeched by, swung in front of her, and pulled in close to the curb.

She jammed on her brakes and barely missed crashing into the truck's back bumper. Breathing deeply to calm herself, she waited for the driver to unload his passenger.

A child jumped down from the cab, a little girl around Megan's age, but more sturdily built and with a mop of black curls. She scooted away, calling back over her shoulder, "'Bye, Dad! Thanks for the drive! See ya!"

The man tooted his horn in response and his truck moved forward, only to stop again sharply with a squeal of brakes.

Kendra had started forward as he did and now she had to brake sharply, too. She felt a twinge of irritation as the driver jumped down from the truck.

"Hey, Jodi!" he yelled. "Isn't this Hot Dog Day?"

"Yikes!" The girl spun round and sped back to him.

He'd walked to the gates and Kendra drummed her fingers on the steering wheel as he whisked out his wallet and hastily handed over a bill. The child raced off again and in a moment had joined the lines filing into the school.

Her father started back toward the truck.

Kendra raked an impatient gaze over him.

He was tall, with wavy black hair; deeply tanned and very attractive in an earthy sort of way. Sexy, with a lean muscular build that was shown off to perfection in narrow-fitting blue jeans and a snug black T-shirt.

He chanced to glance her way and as their eyes met, he grinned, a slanting grin that revealed beautiful teeth, whiter than white.

"Kids." Twinkling eyes fixed on her, he slid his wallet back into his hip pocket. "You've gotta—"

He broke off, his eyes widening, and stopped dead.

He had recognized her...and at exactly the same second as she had recognized him.

She swallowed, and stared back. The air between them seemed to shimmer, the way it always had when she'd looked at him in the past. It was odd and disturbing, and it was something she'd experienced with no other person.

No other man.

Only he hadn't been a man then. He'd been a teenager. Bad and wild and from the wrong side of the tracks.

"Not your kind of boy, missy!"

But she hadn't needed her grandfather to warn her of that. She'd been well aware of it. Of the differences between them.

She wondered now what he was thinking. Were his thoughts paralleling hers? Probably. She'd never made any secret of her disdain for him.

His smile was no longer lazy or friendly, but mocking.

Yes, he remembered...

"Well, now!" With the careless swagger that had been his trademark as a teenager, he moved over to her car. Her nerves seemed to jump as he planted a hand on the Honda's roof and leaned down to her open window. "If it isn't the snooty Westmore brat. Come home to claim her inheritance."

"Well, now, if it isn't that no-good Spencer kid!"

She tilted her chin up and looked straight into eyes that were blue-green and fringed with thick black lashes. "Would you mind moving your old beater, Brodie? I have things to do."

It was only nine o'clock but the September morning was already hot. Kendra became aware that perspiration was rolling down between her breasts, under her yellow tube top.

"Guess you'll be selling the family homestead and taking off again," he drawled. "I heard you got hitched, a while back. Your hubby here in Lakeview with you?"

His gaze dropped to her hands. Her fingers were gripped around the steering wheel. On the left hand, her gold ring glinted. It looked bare. She felt a twinge of unease. Perhaps she should have invested in an engagement ring before coming home; it would have been more...convincing.

Not that she had to convince *this* man of anything!

"Would you mind moving?" she said coolly. "As I said, I have things to—"

"What's your hurry? How about having a coffee with me, for old t—"

She flicked the gear lever into reverse and after a hasty check in the rearview mirror, yanked the Honda back. She heard his startled "Whoa!" as he had to jump aside, and she felt a stab of satisfaction.

Turn signal blinking, she swung out into the street. And then she drove off as fast as she could without actually breaking the speed limit...and without even peeking back once to see if he might be watching.

But as she made her way home, following the Main Street that ran parallel to the lake, the chance meeting lingered in her mind like an unpleasant aftertaste.

It was more than eight years since she'd left the small town of Lakeview in B.C.'s Interior, and in all that time she'd never once given Brodie Spencer a thought. Why should she? He'd never meant anything to her. His father, Danny, had been the Westmore gardener and because Brodie had helped Danny in the summer she'd seen him around the place.

Other than that, because he'd been two years ahead of her in high school, their paths had rarely crossed.

That had suited her just fine!

And it would suit her just as fine, she decided grimly, if that state of affairs was to continue!

The booming Lakeview Construction Company—consisting of offices, lumberyard, warehouses, and store—sprawled over several acres at the east end of Lakeview.

Brodie drove directly there from the school.

After parking his truck in the yard, he jumped down onto the sunbaked dirt and bounded up the wooden steps to the rear entrance.

As he strode along the corridor, he heard voices coming from the office ahead. He recognized Mitzi's breathy tones. When he neared the open door, he heard Pete talking.

"...and she signed the contract Friday. It's a big job, Mitzi."

"I'll put Sam Fleet on it."

"Yeah, Sam can handle it—oh, hi, boss." Pete, the company estimator, nodded to Brodie when he noticed him in the doorway.

Mitzi's bouffant bleached-blond hair swayed as she got to her feet. Stroking down the miniskirt of her white knit dress with its splashy pattern of crimson hearts, she said, "I'll get your coffee, boss."

"Make it an iced tea, Mitzi. Thanks."

As his office manager teetered in her high-heeled sandals to the small lunchroom across the hall, Brodie ambled over to her desk. He picked up a sheaf of papers.

"You were saying, Pete...about a big job?"

"That's it you've got there. For the Westmore place. Rosemount. It's an enormous glitzy property at the west end of the lake, up on the hill. Fantastic view."

"I know it." Brodie was aware that Pete had only been in town six months and didn't know much of its history. "The old guy who owned it passed away recently. Edward Westmore. Made his money way back when, in the stock market. His son Kenneth and his daughter-in-law Sandra both died about twenty years ago. Their daughter—old Westmore's granddaughter—is the one who has inherited the place. So...she's signed up with us, has she?"

"On the dotted line. She wants the kitchen gutted, modernized."

"Is she going to move in...or sell?"

"She's moving in. She wants commercial appliances in the kitchen, she's planning on running Rosemount as a B and B."

As Brodie assimilated that, Pete went on. "She also wants the staircase torn down, and some airy open circular staircase put up in its place—"

"She's going to tear down that mahogany staircase?" Brodie rolled his eyes in disbelief. "The woman's crazy! It's a work of art! Good God, those spindles, that intricate carving—"

"Yeah, I know. I tried to talk her out of it, but she sure put me in my place! She'd been sweet as pie till then, but sheesh! when I put my two cents in—" He slashed his index finger across his throat.

Brodie shook his head. Unbelievable. "I heard Mitzi say she was going to put Sam on the job—"

Mitzi came back into the office and handed him a glass of iced tea. "That's right. Oh, before I forget, boss—Hayley called. She wants you to bring home a half gallon of milk after work. You're clean out and she won't have time to stop in at the supermarket."

"Milk. OK."

"She said to be sure you got fat-free."

Brodie's grin was self-deprecating. "Henpecked, that's what I am! But hey, we all know who's boss in my household!" He gulped down a few mouthfuls of his iced drink and set the glass on Pete's desk. "So...Mitzi, about the Westmore job—have you mentioned it to Sam yet?"

"No, not yet."

"Then don't." Brodie walked to the window and looked out. Even this early the yard was a hive of activity—customers walking among the rows of lumber, men hauling out supplies; trucks coming and going; women browsing in the garden furniture section, taking advantage of the end-of-season sale. He swatted the contract against his thigh. "I'm going to take this one on myself."

"Good luck!" Pete said. "You'll have your hands full dealing with Mrs. Westmore."

"It's not Mrs. Westmore." Brodie's response came absently. "She *was* a Westmore—I don't know what her married name would be though."

"It'll be on the contract." Mitzi took the papers

from Brodie and riffled through them till she found the signature she was looking for.

"Kendra Westmore!" She made a face. "Well, I guess she never did change her name. Some women don't. Me, I can't think why. If you love a man, surely you'd want to bear his name...and have your kids bear his name. 'Course, the reason she and Edward Westmore fell out was because her grandfather disapproved of her intended—at least, that's what folks around here said—and maybe she kept the family name thinking to appease the old man." Mitzi turned to Pete. "Did you meet the husband?"

"Nah, he wasn't around."

"What about kids?" Mitzi asked. "*Does* she have kids? Did you see any when you were out there?"

"She's got a daughter," Pete said. "Spit of herself."

"Well," Mitzi said, "the kid must be pretty as they come. That Westmore girl might have been snooty as all get-out, but she surely was a beauty."

She still is, Brodie thought. She still is!

And he couldn't wait to see the look on her beautiful snooty face when he turned up at her front door tomorrow!

"Megan, you didn't eat your lunch!" Frowning, Kendra took the bulging brown paper bag from her daughter's backpack.

"I'll eat it now, Mom." Megan leaned forward in her chair and stuck out her hand as Kendra made to put the bag in the fridge. "I'm starving!"

"Well no wonder, if you didn't eat at noon!" Kendra slid the lunch bag across the kitchen table.

"It was Hot Dog Day—the homeroom teacher forgot to tell you on Friday that I should bring money.'' Megan opened the bag and took out a cheese-filled English muffin. ''But my new friend had extra money—she was late this morning and was in a hurry and her dad gave her too much—so she paid for my hot dog and chocolate milk. She said I could pay for hers next time around.''

At the words ''new friend'' Kendra had felt a swift kick of relief. She'd worried about Megan starting over again in a school where most eight-year olds would already have their own special buddies; it seemed she'd had no need to fret. But then at the words ''she was late...and her Dad gave her too much,'' her nerves prickled a warning.

''So,'' she said casually, ''what's your friend's name?''

''Jodi. She's my age and she's got black curly hair...''

But Kendra was no longer listening. She didn't have to. She knew the rest.

Of all the luck, Megan had to link up with Brodie Spencer's daughter! If she was anything like her father, she'd be bad news, and likely to lead Megan into all sorts of trouble—

Oh, she was being ridiculous! This was only Megan's first day at school. She would meet other girls, become friendly with other girls. More suitable girls. Water always found its own level.

''I'll give you money for her tomorrow,'' she said.

''But Mom—''

''You know I don't like you to borrow. But it was kind of this Jodi to help you out. However, you'll pay her back in the morning and that'll be the end of it. All right?''

Megan shrugged. "OK." She concentrated on eating her muffin. "But I hope I don't hurt her feelings," she mumbled. "She's really nice. And she's already asked me to come to her house on Saturday afternoon to play."

"You know you're not allowed to make that kind of arrangement without discussing it with me first!"

Her tone must have been unusually sharp because Megan's head shot up, her brown eyes wide with astonishment. "I didn't! But she's got a brother and a sister and a dog and a swimming pool and her house seems like it's just the funnest place to be!"

Kendra sat down at the table.

"Honey," she said carefully, "don't be in too much of a hurry to make a special friend. It's a mistake lots of people make. Take your time, get to know *everybody* first. And then make up your mind who you like."

"When you were my age," Megan challenged, "did your mother pick and choose your friends?"

"I lost my parents when I was six. I've told you many times, sweetie, that my grandfather Westmore brought me up. And though he didn't pick and choose my friends, he did try to make sure that my choices were...the right ones."

"Well, why don't we have Jodi over *here* on Saturday? Then you can see for yourself if she's a right choice!"

Trapped. She felt trapped. Yet wasn't what Megan was suggesting a sensible plan? How could she get out of it, without seeming totally unreasonable!

"It's just Monday," she said. "Why don't we wait till the end of the week, see how it goes? Perhaps you'll meet someone else you'd rather invite here on Saturday."

"Sure." Megan reached for the bottle of orange juice. "Let's wait till Friday."

Kendra heaved a sigh of relief.

But it was short-lived.

"I can tell you now, though," Megan said as she popped off the lid and stuck a straw into the bottle, "that I won't be meeting anybody I'll like better than Jodi Spencer!"

The wall phone rang before Kendra could come up with a response. Pushing back her chair, she reached for the receiver. "Westmore residence."

"Good afternoon, Ms. Westmore. This is Mitzi, at Lakeview Construction. Someone will be coming out tomorrow morning to talk with you about your new kitchen. Will eight-thirty be too early?"

"No, eight-thirty will be fine. Thanks."

She hung up.

"Finished your snack?" she asked Megan.

"Yes, I'm done."

"Let's get our bikes then and cycle down to the school. I want to be sure we have your route all mapped out because I won't be able to drive you in the morning. I have to be here, to talk to the workman from Lakeview Construction."

"Full fat!" The hem of Hayley Spencer's shortie robe fluttered around her sun-browned thighs as she swirled around from the fridge, half-gallon milk jug held aloft. Rolling her eyes, she set the jug on the breakfast table. "I'm trying to lose weight and the man buys me full fat milk!"

She lowered herself into her chair and pouring bran

flakes into a blue-rimmed bowl, called after Brodie, who was headed for the door, "I told Ditsy Mitzi fat-free! Why don't you fire the woman and hire somebody who can take a simple message!"

Brodie paused in the doorway and looked round with an apologetic grin. "Mitzi did mention it...and you know damned well she's not ditsy—she just *looks* ditsy! The fault is mine. I guess I had other things on my mind yesterday." *Like the Westmore woman!* "It won't happen again—"

He stepped aside smartly as Jodi and her brother bowled by in tandem, Jodi in pretty pink dungarees and a candy-striped blouse, Jack in a grungy gray T-shirt and baggy shorts. The boy had combed his black hair in a middle part and plastered it to his skull with foul-smelling gunk. Brodie's nostrils quivered, but he bit back a dry comment. He knew only too well how much Jack loathed his unruly curls. He had, too, when he'd been that age—too young to know that when he became a teenager, girls would find his hair irresistible! His lips twitched at the memory...

"Morning, kids," he said.

"Morning, Dad." Jodi threw him a cheery smile.

"Yo." Jack had already thrown himself onto a chair and was grabbing his favorite cereal packet.

"How come you're dressed so fine?" Jodi's gaze flicked over him even as she reached for a bowl. "Aren't you going in to the yard this morning?"

"He's going to the Westmore place." Hayley's lovely cornflower blue eyes had the same inquisitive glint as Jodi's, but added to that was a speculative gleam as she looked at his emerald polo shirt and neatly pressed chinos.

"If you're going out there," Jodi said, "will you do me a favor, Dad?"

Brodie glanced at his watch. "Look, I've gotta run—"

"There's a new girl in my class. I forgot to tell you last night. She's Megan Westmore. She's got no brothers or sisters so I asked her to come over on Saturday afternoon. She said she'd ask her mom. But *you* can ask her today!"

Hayley frowned. "Jodi, you know Saturday afternoon is a family time for us."

"If you've already asked her," Brodie said, "we'll have to follow up on it."

Hayley's slender shoulders lifted in a shrug. "Yes, I suppose..."

But Brodie could feel her disapproval emanating from across the kitchen. He glanced at his watch. He should really be out of here!

He strode to the table and leaning over Hayley, planted a quick kiss on the tip of her nose. "Don't worry, Hayle, her mother probably won't let her come."

As he left, he caught himself glancing around the kitchen—assessingly; something he hadn't done in a very long time. The big square room was bright and cheerful and airy...and shabby. He'd always liked it that way...but this was undoubtedly a house where things were neglected.

From the beginning, he'd wanted to hire a housekeeper, but Hayley wouldn't hear of it. He'd given in, and had never regretted the decision.

But minutes later, as he started his truck, he found himself wondering how the place would look to the snooty Ms. Westmore. And admitted it would come up short. The kitchen badly needed redecorating, as did the rest of the modest two-story house. What was that adage about the shoemaker's kids having no shoes? It certainly fit in his case.

But hell, his decision to keep things as they were hadn't been grounded in laziness. It had been grounded in a desire to give the kids stability. To give them a sense that, although a lot of things had changed, their roots would never.

Were they old enough now to accept change?

They'd been through so much.

But maybe it was time to throw them a challenge.

Maybe, after he'd finished with the Westmore project, he'd tackle instituting some changes at home.

Bit by bit. So the changes wouldn't come all at once and be too distressing for them.

Yeah, he decided as he followed the road that led out of town toward Rosemount, one step at a time.

That was the answer.

Kendra was out back, getting Megan's bike from the shed, when she heard the roar of a truck coming up the drive at the front of the house.

At the same time, Megan shot out through the kitchen door. She looked fresh and sweet in an ice-blue jumpsuit.

"Got everything, honey?" Kendra asked.

"Yes."

"And you know the way? Along the—"

"Mom, we did that yesterday!" Impatiently, Megan grabbed the bike handles. "Thanks." She jumped on the mountain bike and took off across the white gravel chips, her tires crunching. "'Bye, Mom! See you after school!"

"'Bye, honey! Take care..."

Kendra watched till her daughter disappeared around the corner of the house. Then she turned, letting her gaze sweep up over the enormous white mansion that had stood here, on top of the hill, for more than sixty years.

The breeze riffled pleasantly through her hair and the sun kissed her cheeks. She smiled and tucked her hands into the pockets of her white shorts as she walked toward the open back door. She was glad to be home. More than glad: elated! When her grandfather had thrown her out eight years ago, she'd left her heart in Lakeview. Now she was back, she would never leave again. No matter what.

She crossed the kitchen, walked along the corridor, and paused for a moment when she reached the foyer.

Sunlight flooded down from the tall window in the stairwell, its mellow rays glowing on the Persian rug and parquet floor. Sunlight gleamed, too, on the polished mahogany furniture, and enriched the opulent color of the tapestries adorning the walls. The staircase itself was the hall's focal point, its elegant lines and luxurious blue runner drawing the eye up to the landing.

As a child she'd never been tempted to slide down the smooth banister...but Megan seemed to find it irresistible. Kendra was well aware that despite being cautioned several times to keep off it, the child still sailed recklessly, joyfully down it when her mother wasn't around.

An accident waiting to happen—

The front doorbell clanged.

Kendra turned and crossed the foyer, and as she did, she found herself wondering if it wouldn't be better to postpone the kitchen project and deal with the staircase first. Yes, that's what she would do. And as soon as it was replaced, she could stop worrying…

Content with her decision, she opened the front door.

And came face-to-face with a man she had hoped never to bump into again. He was dressed to kill and she could smell the faintest hint of a musky aftershave over the sweet scent of roses drifting from a nearby flower bed.

"Brodie Spencer!" She rammed her hands on her hips and glared at him. "What on earth are *you* doing here!"

CHAPTER TWO

"A SIMPLE 'Good morning,'" Brodie returned innocently, "would have sufficed!"

His lips twitched as he saw her gaze become even more belligerent. Boy, she sure was something else when she got mad! Sparks exploded like fireworks in her brown eyes, and her breasts quivered! Yup, quivered. Under that cobalt blue tank top, they quivered.

"I said—" her voice was icy "—what do you want?'

He cleared his throat and jerked his gaze back to her face. What did he want? Hell, she wouldn't like his honest answer to *that* question. No, sirree!

"Lakeview Construction at your service, ma'am."

She stared at him blankly for a full seven seconds...which gave him time to scrutinize her hair. It hung loose this morning, the heavy blunt-cut tips brushing her tanned shoulders, and each strand glistened as if it had been individually dipped in white gold. He felt a strong urge to reach out and run his fingers through—

She made a sound that reminded him of a piglet's snort.

"You're kidding," she said scathingly. "Of course."

"No, ma'am. I am not." He pressed his right hand flat against his heart. And noticed it was beating just a tad faster than usual. "I'm here to discuss your...kitchen."

He saw the incredulity in her eyes.

He showed her the work order.

She scrutinised it but when she handed it back, her expression had become only marginally less hostile.

"You'd better come inside." She made no secret of her reluctance to invite him into the house. And she flounced away, leaving him to close the door behind him. The rich, it seemed, did not always have impeccable manners!

She halted in the middle of the foyer and turned to him. She'd schooled her features into an emotionless mask.

"There's been a change in plan," she said. "I want to postpone work on the kitchen and start with the staircase."

Brodie smelled coffee.

He'd been in such an all-fired rush that morning he hadn't taken time to have his usual caffeine fix. He sure could do with it now, to set him up before he got down to the nitty-gritty of telling his client she'd be a fool to tear down her magnificent antique mahogany staircase.

"Let's talk about that," he said smoothly. "Over...a coffee, maybe?"

He could feel her irritation coming at him in waves. But she said, albeit stiffly, "All right."

She took off along the corridor to the left of the foyer, and he followed like a sheep.

Except that a sheep wouldn't have ogled her derriere the way he was doing—well, how could he not? It was sexy as hell in those skimpy white shorts—and she still walked with that tantalizing little wiggle of her hips, the way she'd done when she was a teenager!

"You can see," she said as he entered the kitchen behind her, "why I want this room modernized."

He glanced around and murmured in agreement. The cupboards were faced with outdated Formica, the appliances were ancient and an unfashionable olive green, the linoleum so old the pattern was worn away in places, and the lighting fixtures pathetically inadequate. Yup, he thought, it would be a pleasure to gut this place out and start from scratch!

He returned his attention to the woman walking to the countertop by the sink, and watched her reach up to a side cupboard for two mugs.

She was in front of the window, and backlit against the brilliant sunshine. All he could see of her was her shape—her slim shoulders, her hand-span waist, her curvy hips.

She had some gorgeous figure!

"How do you like it?" Her voice came to him through a scarlet mist of lust.

"Oh, I like it just fine!" he said.

"I beg your pardon?"

Her frosty tone jarred him out of his carnal fantasies. "Ah, the...er...coffee. Black'll be just fine. Thank you, ma'am."

She didn't invite him to sit, so he leaned back against the countertop, ankles casually crossed.

She stood, like a robot, with her hands cupped around her mug, the steam rising so that her face seemed to shimmer.

OK, he thought, time to get this over with.

He leveled a steady look at her luminous brown eyes, with their luxuriant fringe of wheat-blond lashes.

"Your husband," he said. "Does he agree with you about tearing down the staircase?"

He saw her fingers tighten around her mug. "I'm a widow, Mr. Spencer. Every decision I make is my own."

A widow. So the lovely little heiress hadn't had it quite as easy as he'd thought.

"Sorry to hear it." And he was. Being a single parent was a tough row to hoe. "Must be lonely for you. How long is it since..."

"Six years."

The answer came out as reluctantly as if he'd forced it at gunpoint! "And you've been living...where? Vancouver?"

"Yes."

"Did you graduate...from U.B.C.?"

"No. I wanted to stay home when Megan was a baby."

"You were fortunate to have that choice. And now...well, you still have that choice—to be a lady of leisure...as you pretty much would be, with Megan in school. But Pete tells me you're planning to run this place as a B and B. Surprised the hell out of me—"

"I'm not a parasite, Brodie." Anger flared in her eyes. "I want the satisfaction of knowing that I'm earning the money my child and I will be living on. And while we're on the subject of money, there's something I'd like to clear up. Your daughter loaned Megan some money yesterday, for hot dogs. I've had a talk with Megan about this—she's been brought up never to lend or borrow. I gave her money this morning to repay the loan—"

"No problem." He waved her words aside. "Glad Jodi could help."

"The point I'm making is that I don't want it to happen again." A vein pulsed at her temple. "In the future, if Megan doesn't bring lunch money, she'll have to go hungry."

Brodie got the distinct feeling that there was more to this than seemed on the surface. Like a dentist who suspects a tooth may not be as healthy as it looks, he decided to probe.

"Jodi tells me she's invited Megan to spend this Saturday afternoon with our family. I'm supposed to confirm that she can come."

"Megan mentioned something of the kind." A pink flush colored her cheekbones. "I've told her we'll discuss it on Friday. She's only just started school here. I don't want her to...rush...anything..." Her voice trailed away, but her chin came up in a stubborn tilt.

There it was, then; a crack in the beautiful white enamel. And...something rotten underneath?

"Ah," he said. "In case a better offer comes up."

The flush in her cheeks deepened till her skin was as red as ripe raspberries. "That's not what I said."

"No, that's not what you *said.*"

God, he could hardly believe it. But he might have known. Despite being an adult now, the Westmore brat—the Westmore *Widow!*—was just as much a snob as she'd been at seventeen. No way was she going to allow her precious daughter to become friends with Brodie Spencer's kid.

No way.

It was Jodi he felt sorry for. She'd seemed very taken with this new girl. She was going to be mighty disappointed—and hurt—when she discovered that Megan Westmore was forbidden to play with her.

Dammit, he detested snobbery!

He slammed his mug down on the table.

"Right!" he said. "We know where we both stand. So let's not waste any more of each other's time on it. Let's get back to business! You want us to rip down that staircase? Fine, we'll rip it down. The only problem is that the replacement you told my estimator you wanted—white-enameled wrought-iron—is back-ordered and won't be available till late October. So in the meantime, we'll do the kitchen. I'll get a couple of men up here this afternoon and we'll get the project under way. You realize you'll be without a kitchen in the meantime?"

"Yes." The raspberry color had seeped from her face; now it looked pale as cream. "Megan and I will use the kitchenette in what used to be the servants' quarters. You'll just have to let me know when you'll be shutting off the water, electricity, and so on, so I can work around it."

"You'll need to choose new cupboards, appliances, floor covering, wall tiles, paint..." His gesture was wide. "Come down to the store sometime, just call first and set up an appointment and I'll show you around. Give you advice."

He sensed her hackles rise when he mentioned giving her advice.

"You do that, too?" she asked. "As well as the...donkey work?"

The hands that had itched to reach out and touch her hair a few minutes ago now itched to reach out and wrap themselves around her pretty little throat.

"Yes," he said in a gritty voice. "As well as doing

the donkey work I do, on occasion, dole out advice.''
If he stayed, he knew he'd say, or do, something he'd regret, so he excused himself and made for the door.

As he strode angrily out to the foyer, he knew exactly what she was thinking: Hell will freeze over, Brodie Spencer, before I ever seek advice from you!

Dammit! he thought. She was the most infuriating woman he'd ever met...and the most arrogant. But he'd knock that arrogance out of her, one way or another, if it was the very last thing he ever did.

Kendra managed to hold herself together till she heard the front door slam behind him.

Then she sank down on the nearest chair, her mug still clutched in her hands. She realized she was shaking. Taking a long gulp of her coffee, she stared blindly into space and tried to sort out her thoughts.

What *was* it about this man that disturbed her so deeply? Was it the physicality of him? The earthiness? The sexy aura he emanated? Or was it his mocking tone, the cocky arrogance he revealed in her presence? He never really did or said anything out of place...yet it was always there, under the surface. The... *battle*...between them.

And somehow he always came out on top.

This thing with the Saturday invitation. She was perfectly within her rights to turn it down, and she had no obligation to give a reason. Why then was she the one left feeling...guilty?

Darn it! She put down her mug, shoved back her chair. She was not going to spend any more time with this man, she was not going to allow him in her house again. She wanted to live in Lakeview, and she wanted it to be a peaceful haven. She knew she could build a good life here, for herself and Megan.

But Brodie Spencer was in the way!

He needled, and he pushed buttons, and he made her downright...uncomfortable.

And she wasn't going to take it anymore!

She lurched to her feet and crossed to the desk.

She'd thought she'd placed her copy of the Lakeview Construction contract on top, but it wasn't there! Where on earth had she put it?

It took her several minutes to discover it had fallen to the floor, behind the desk.

She set it on the table and ran a finger down the page till she found what she was looking for. Swinging around, she crossed to the wall phone and punched in the number.

"Lakeview Construction," came a breathy voice. "Mitzi speaking."

"Mitzi, this is Kendra Westmore—"

"What's wrong, Ms. Westmore? Didn't Brodie turn up?"

"Oh, yes, he turned up all right. The problem is—"

"Problem? You have a problem?"

"It's not going to work out. He's not going to work out. I mean...what I mean is, I can't work with the man. I want someone else to be put in charge of the project."

"But Brodie's—"

"No ifs, ands, or buts. I want another—"

She heard a kerfuffle at the other end of the line. Then she heard muffled voices. In the background.

"Hello?" Exasperation made her voice shrill. "Hello? Mitzi? What's going on?"

"Hi."

Oh, she knew that voice. Brodie must have gone straight back to the office. Probably to complain about her attitude! Well, great. That worked both ways. He didn't want her, she didn't want him, either!

"Let me talk to your boss," she fairly hissed. "Now!"

He chuckled, and anger spilled through her.

"Brodie, I'm warning you—"

"You want to talk to the boss?"

"Finally you've got it!"

"The boss of Lakeview Construction? The owner, manager, chairman, and president?" His words were threaded with laughter.

"Yes!" she exploded.

"You're talkin' to him!" All of a sudden she heard a grimness in his tone, a steely note that hadn't been there before. "Brodie Spencer owns the company, lock, stock, and barrel. He's the man who makes all the decisions, and he's the man who's going to head your project. We have a contract, you and I. A contract that's iron-clad. You may not like it but you're stuck with it. You may not like me—and it's clear that you don't—but you're stuck with me, too. So you'd better get used to seeing me around, *ma'am,* because that's the way it's going to be!"

Kendra spent the rest of the morning cleaning out the kitchen and carting everything from there to the kitchenette.

It lay along the corridor from the kitchen, just beyond the mudroom and the swing door that separated the main part of the house from the servants' quarters.

The servants' quarters hadn't been used any time

in Kendra's memory. Her grandmother had apparently been 'delicate,' and had required live-in help; but after his wife's death Edward Westmore had let the housekeeper go, along with the several housemaids. From then on, he'd depended on a local woman who came in daily to cook and clean. Molly Flynn was surly and unpleasant. Kendra had disliked her intensely, so when the woman phoned Rosemount the day after Edward Westmore's funeral to say she wouldn't be coming in anymore, Kendra had breathed a sigh of relief that she was spared the task of firing her.

Now this morning, as she busied herself emptying the kitchen so the workmen could get started, she was alone. Alone in body, but not in mind, because as she worked, Brodie Spencer kept intruding on her thoughts, no matter how she tried to keep him at bay.

And always the image was vivid: blue-green eyes glinting with mockery; sensual lips curled tauntingly; magnificent male body exuding arrogant challenge and blatant sexual charisma from every muscle, bone, and pore.

Oh, how she hated the man!

Shoving open the swing door with her hip, she marched into the kitchenette with the very last load, and thumped the tray of dishes down on the scrubbed pine table with such force that the delicate china plates trembled.

There, that was it. *Finito.*

Now Lakeview Construction could get on with the job.

Flinging open the window, she curled her hands around the edge of the sink and stared out over the gravelled parking area.

Bad enough, she reflected irritably, that she was

going to have to endure having Brodie Spencer in her home for the next few weeks; but that wasn't the only thing gnawing away at her. The awkward situation with his daughter and Megan had been niggling at her, too.

What if Friday rolled around and Megan hadn't found another friend? What if she still wanted to spend Saturday afternoon with Jodi Spencer?

Perhaps, though, after this morning's confrontation, Brodie would be as much against the looming liaison as she was. Perhaps he'd try to steer Jodi away from Megan—

And where would his wife fit into all of this?

It suddenly struck Kendra that if Jodi and Megan were in the same grade at school, they must be approximately the same age. That meant that Brodie must have become a father when he was only nineteen.

She frowned.

He'd been a hellion in those days, ripping around on his motorbike—black leather jacket, wicked grin, the whole nine yards. The clichéd "bad boy," always in some kind of trouble. And "bad boys" didn't turn into family men at nineteen...

Unless...yes, he probably got some girl pregnant.

Probably got himself trapped.

Kendra felt a faint flicker of curiosity. What was she like, Brodie Spencer's wife? And where did the family live? If Brodie owned Lakeview Construction, in all likelihood he'd have built himself a fancy new house. Possibly it was one of those modern mansions she'd seen north of Lakeview Road, as she'd driven into town ten days ago when she'd come home for her grandfather's funeral...

She sighed, and hugged her arms around herself.

Her grandfather.

She could still scarcely believe he was gone.

And she could still scarcely believe he had left her everything. Not only Rosemount, but all his money. She'd assumed that when he had written her out of his life, he had written her out of his will, too.

She had been mistaken.

Once she'd gotten over her shock, she'd given in her notice at the small hotel where she worked as a chef; spent the next twenty-four hours disposing of her meager household possessions; and then had driven, with Megan, to Lakeview.

She'd been glad to get out of the city.

And filled with growing joy at the prospect of bringing Megan up in the town where she had herself grown up.

She had always loved Lakeview. It had never occurred to her that once there, she'd find a fly in the ointment.

Brodie Spencer!

And speak of pesky flies! she thought as a familiar red truck appeared around the side of the house and pulled up a few yards from the kitchen door. This one was back!

As Brodie jumped down from the cab, a blue van came into sight and spun to a halt, its rear wheels scattering white gravel chips into the air.

Two men emerged. Both wore checked shirts, heavy-duty jeans, workboots. Brodie himself had changed and looked more ruggedly sexy than ever in beat-up jeans, a sun-faded denim shirt, and heavy leather boots.

The two men followed Brodie as he strode to the door.

Squaring her shoulders, Kendra went to let them in.

One day at a time, she told herself. Take it one day at a time.

"What are you doing here, Mom?" Megan scowled as she walked her bike over to her mother. "I know my way home!"

Kendra moved her own bike back to let some children scuffle past her through the school gates. "I just had to get out of the house! There's such a racket, workmen tearing down cupboards and—"

"Hey, Jodi," Megan called. "Wait up!"

Kendra suddenly noticed the Spencer child a few yards away on the sidewalk. She was wheeling her bike towards the road. The girl turned and shouted to Megan, "Can't! I gotta go!" And with that, she threw herself onto her bike and pedaled away like mad along the street.

Megan yelled after her, "But you said—" She broke off as she realized that Jodi was now too far away to hear.

Pouting, Megan looked at her mother. "If you hadn't turned up, Jodi was going to take me to the rec center. The dance teacher's going to be signing up new members for beginners' jazz, and I wanted to put my name down."

"Jazz? But what about your ballet? I thought—"

"I can do both. Jodi's in jazz and ballet and tap."

Megan's determined tone made it quite clear to Kendra that keeping the two girls apart wasn't going to be easy.

"And don't say we can't afford it!" Megan's

cheeks had become flushed. "Maybe we couldn't before, when we had to watch our pennies...but you hit the jackpot big-time when your granddaddy died and—"

"Hit the jackpot?" Kendra stared at her daughter. "Big-time? When my granddaddy died? Young lady, if that's the kind of talk you're hearing from Jodi Spencer, you can forget about jazz lessons, and Saturday outings to the Spencer place—in fact, you can just forget having anything to do with that girl! And we're going home. Right now!"

Megan muttered something under her breath.

"What did you say?"

"It wasn't Jodi. At least, she just told me what she heard...somebody else...saying."

And who might that somebody else have been? Kendra thought bitterly. There was only one answer to that.

"Let's go!" she snapped.

Megan did get on her bike, and she did ride home with her mother. In body, if not in spirit. But as soon as they were inside, she headed for the stairs.

"Where are you going?" Kendra asked.

"Up to my room to do my homework."

"Don't you want a snack?"

"I'm not hungry."

"We'll eat at five, then. In the kitchenette. I'll call you once the men have gone home for the day."

Darn it, she thought as Megan took off up the stairs, the last thing she wanted to do was fight with her daughter. Sighing, she crossed the foyer and made for the servants' quarters.

She could hear, up ahead, the whine of a chainsaw. Bangs and crashes. Voices and loud music. Laughter.

She was walking along the shadowy corridor past the kitchen when the door swung open and Brodie came out.

They collided with a thump and she was thrown wildly off balance. He lunged after her and grabbed her upper arms to pull her upright and steady her.

She felt his fingers bruising her flesh, felt his warm breath on her cheeks. His hands smelled of fresh wood shavings and his body smelled of not-so-fresh sweat—a musky male odor that should have been repellent but instead was disturbing in a dark and primal way.

"You OK?" he asked.

"Yes." Her voice was stiff.

He released her. "Sorry, I wasn't looking where I was going."

"It was just as much my fault." She made to move on.

"Before you go—"

"Yes?"

"About Saturday."

She tensed. And waited.

"How about if we include you in the invitation? That way you'll get to see for yourself what we're all about. The Spencer family, that is." His eyes had a hard gleam. "Just because you and I can't get along doesn't mean our kids can't be friends. And I believe it's important that children be allowed to choose their own friends—unless there's good reason to interfere."

She met his gaze stubbornly. "As I told you, Megan and I have agreed to wait till Friday before she decides."

"Meanwhile Jodi sits back and cools her heels?"

''She's perfectly at liberty to withdraw the invitation.''

''Oh, you'd like that, wouldn't you! But that's not the way our family operates. The invitation stands.''

Kendra shrugged. ''Then we'll just have to wait till Friday to find out what Megan decides.''

''What Megan decides...or what her *mother* decides?''

Irritably, she sidestepped him and walked away.

His cynical laugh followed her to the kitchenette, and echoed in her head long after he and his men had left for the day.

CHAPTER THREE

BRODIE got home from work that afternoon around five-thirty. Jodi was sitting on the front step, and when he jumped down from the truck, she ran over to meet him.

"Hi, Dad, I've been waiting for you." She slipped her hand in his and they walked together to the picket gate that led to the back of the house. It snapped shut behind them as they stepped along the cement path. "Did you talk to Megan's mom?" she asked eagerly. "About Saturday?"

"Yeah," he said, "I talked with her."

"And what did she say?"

In the backyard, Hayley was climbing out of the pool. She was wearing a black bikini that showed off her summer tan. She scooped up a towel and, running it through her waist-length brown hair, walked over to join them.

"Hi, Hayle," he said. "How was your day?"

"Busy...but OK." She wrapped the towel casually around her hips. "Dinner'll be ready in half an hour."

"Dad!" Jodi tugged the rolled-up sleeve of his denim shirt. "Is Megan coming on Saturday or what?"

"We won't know till Friday."

"Oh." She wrinkled her nose. "That's what Megan said. Her mom told her she had to not rush in and make best friends on her first day at school. I guess it makes sense.'' But her sigh let him know how disappointed she was.

''Fingers crossed,'' he said. ''And I invited her mom to come, too, so she can get to know us.''

After a beat, Hayley asked, ''What's she like?''

''Oh, she's really neat!'' Jodi said. ''She enjoys most of the things I do—dancing, and math, and Barbies, and—''

''I meant the mother.'' Hayley slipped her feet into the floral thongs she'd left on the patio, and looked at Brodie.

Sensing that Jodi had her ears perked, and that whatever he said would in all likelihood be repeated to Megan at the first opportunity, Brodie replied blandly, ''She's very pleasant.'' *And pigs can sing!*

''Is she pretty?'' Hayley tugged open the screen door.

''According to Mitzi,'' he said evasively, ''Kendra Westmore is drop-dead gorgeous.''

''But what do *you* think?'' Hayley held the door open and her cornflower blue eyes seemed to laser right into him.

''Yeah.'' He lifted his wide shoulders in a careless shrug. ''The lady is indeed more than passably attractive.''

''Mmm.'' The cornflower blue eyes became thoughtful.

But Hayley didn't pursue the matter.

Not then; and not over dinner.

But later, as he was helping her with the washing up, she said in an offhand tone, ''I hope the Westmore woman does decide to come over on Saturday.'' She avoided his eyes as she handed him a pot to dry. ''If

Jodi and Megan are to become friends, then it would be a good thing to get to know the mother, too.''

Brodie had never understood the working of Hayley's mind. The female mind. What man ever did understand the workings of such an intricate mechanism! But he had the disturbing feeling that Hayley was up to something. He had no idea what it was; and he knew better than to ask.

All would be revealed, he had no doubt, in the fullness of time.

Next morning Kendra was out back, having just watched Megan cycle off to school, when Brodie's truck rumbled around the corner.

Though feeling defensive after their last encounter, she resisted the urge to scurry away. Instead she stood her ground, and slipping her hands into the pockets of her airy summer skirt, she waited for him to approach.

He was wearing a black T-shirt and khaki shorts and heavy workboots that crunched on the gravel as he walked. The man, she reflected bleakly, was all tan and muscle and hard male arrogance.

But she wasn't the only one doing the looking. He was giving her a thorough once-over, his deliberate gaze taking in the sleek swing of her blond hair; the swell of her breasts under her tank top; and the slender length of her legs, revealed to him in all their shapely glory as a gust of wind plastered the full skirt to her thighs.

She felt as exposed as if she'd been naked but she refused to adjust the thin fabric, knowing that if she did he would see her discomfiture...and gloat over it.

She tilted her head regally. ''Since you're going to

be in and out a lot you ought to have a key to the back door.'' She drew the spare key from the pocket where she'd stored it. ''That way, when I'm not around, you can come and go as you please.''

''Thanks.'' He took the key and shoved it into his hip pocket. ''So...why so sour this beautiful morning? Bad hair day? No—'' his gaze drifted over her hair ''—can't be that. No sirree.''

The sudden heat in her cheeks wasn't due to the sun. With fake pleasantry, she said, ''Brodie, our relationship is a strictly business one. If you don't want to be sued for sexual harassment, you'll avoid making comments like that.''

He raised his eyebrows. ''Can't a man pay a simple compliment these days without ending up in court?''

''In a business situation,'' she said in a supercilious tone, ''personal comments are totally out of place.''

''Mmm. Am I to understand then that if you and your daughter accept our *family* invitation on Saturday, I'll be free to express my admiration for any part of your anatomy which attracts my attention?''

Through gritted teeth, she muttered, ''That's not what I said!''

''How about if we ever go out on a date, then? Just the two of us? Would it be OK then?''

The man was married, for heaven's sake, with children. But even if he'd been single and the most eligible bachelor in town, she wouldn't have considered going out with him. He hadn't changed one bit—he was still the same incorrigible flirt he'd been as a teenager!

''Yes.'' Her voice was honey-sweet. ''It would be OK then. But since I shall never go out on a date with you, Brodie, the question doesn't…nor ever will…arise."

"Never say never."

"Oh, I can say it and with more conviction than I've ever said anything in my life. I shall never—read my lips, Mr. Spencer—*never* go out on a date with you."

She swirled away from him and made for the back door.

But as she stalked into the house she heard him call after her in that mocking tone that had already become so familiar.

"Famous last words, Ms. Westmore. Famous last words."

Kendra resolved to keep out of his way for the rest of the day, but their altercation had left her strangely restless and she itched to busy herself with something.

In the end, she decided to work in the garden—the front garden, out of sight and sound of the kitchen.

She was on her hands and knees, weeding a rose bed, when a mail van came up the drive. She leaned back on her heels as the driver jumped out—a man in his mid-twenties.

He seemed vaguely familiar.

"Hi!" He walked over to her and slipped a couple of fliers from his bag. "Long time no see, Kendra!"

Blue Jamieson. She'd known him in high school—and she remembered what a struggle he'd had in school because he'd had a learning disability. She also remembered how immensely likable he'd been.

She'd known his father, too. Ben Jamieson had been the Westmore family doctor.

Kendra swallowed hard as she recalled the last time

she'd sat in Dr. Jamieson's office. Christmas Eve. Eight years past. It had been the worst day of her life.

Bar none.

"Well, hi yourself, Blue!" She scrambled to her feet and took the fliers. "Long time no see indeed!"

"Doing your own gardening now, huh? The Kendra I knew wouldn't have dirtied her pretty little hands!" His ingenuous smile took any sting out of his words. "What's up? You on a budget?"

She laughed. "No, no budget. I just haven't hired a gardener yet, though my ad should be in the *Lakeview Gazette* today. Apparently my grandfather used a gardening company the past six years but I don't want to go that route."

"Yeah, Mr. Westmore started using the gardening company after Danny Spencer died. What a tragedy that was—you've heard about it, of course."

"No. What happened?"

"Danny's son Jack and Jack's wife Maureen drove the old guy down to Vancouver on his sixty-fifth birthday—for some special hockey game he wanted to see—"

"I didn't know Brodie had a brother."

"Oh, yeah. Jack was fifteen years older than Brodie, a real nice guy. Worked in the Royal Bank. Anyway, on the way back from Vancouver, they ran into a snowstorm and were involved in a big smash on the Coquihalla—some truck lost its brakes and rammed into Jack's Pinto. They were all killed. Well, Danny hung on for a week or so, but..."

Kendra felt goose bumps rise on her arms. "How awful."

"Folks say only one good thing came out of that

accident. It sure brought out the best in Brodie Spencer—''

''Hey, Blue, you taking my name in vain?''

They both turned and saw Brodie walking across the lawn, a mug in one hand. He was still yards away, and couldn't have heard much more than just his name.

Blue smoothed over what could have been an awkward moment by saying, ''Just reminding Kendra of the old days, Brodie...when you were hell on wheels! You were the envy of all us guys when you bought your Harley-Davidson motorcycle.''

''Kendra's grandfather gave me the money for that bike!''

Before Kendra could protest, he went on, dryly, ''Of course, I had to work my butt off in his gardens for three summers to make it!''

Blue laughed. ''Yeah, you did that, Brodie. While the rest of us guys were goofing off at the lake and having fun. Well—'' he turned ''—I gotta go! Great seeing you, Kendra!''

After he'd left, Brodie lingered.

''Yes?'' She rolled up the fliers Blue had given her, and curled a tight hand around them. ''What do you want?''

''Just taking my break, decided to get some air.'' He raised his eyebrows. ''Any objections to the hired hand coming around the front to drink his coffee?''

''Why do you take such a perverse delight in needling me?''

His laugh was without humor. ''Delight? I take no delight in it!''

''Then why do you do it, Brodie? What do you hope to achieve?''

"I don't really *hope* to achieve anything! But what I'd *like* to achieve is...to find out what makes you tick!"

"Why on earth would that interest you? Besides, I'm a very simple person. Easy to read, easy to understand. There's no mystery about me, Brodie. I have no secrets."

Now there was a lie if ever there was one! And if Brodie Spencer were ever to discover her secret—

Her heart shuddered.

But he never would.

She didn't know it all herself! And that was a bitter irony. It was like a puzzle with all the pieces in place...except one. The biggest piece.

The piece that was integral to solving the puzzle.

But it had gotten torn in two.

She had one half.

And she didn't know who had the other.

It was a nightmare from which there was no awakening.

A nightmare she'd lived with for more than eight years, and was probably doomed to live with forever—

"Did Megan's father understand you?"

"What?"

Brodie's gaze had narrowed. "You say you're easy to read. Did your husband understand you?"

She suppressed a bark of hysterical laughter. Brodie's expression would be a picture if she confessed the truth.

The scandalous truth.

"Yes," she said. "He understood me perfectly."

Brodie was looking at her hands and she suddenly realized she was plucking at the fliers; ripping off scraps, letting them fall like confetti to the grass. How long had she been doing it? Jerking in a quick breath, she stilled her fingers. And hoped Brodie hadn't guessed he'd hit a raw nerve.

But perhaps he had, and perhaps he regretted it because when he spoke again it was in a neutral tone.

"Look," he said, "what I really came out for was—I need you to come along to the kitchen. We've hit a…snag."

"What kind of a snag?"

"I'd like to show you."

They crossed the lawn together, their shadows mingling on the bright green grass. A bee buzzed around Brodie's head, and he swatted it away. From the kitchen window came the beat of a stereo.

When they reached the open door, Brodie stood back to let her enter first. Then he crossed to the ghetto blaster set on the wide windowsill above the sink, and switched it off. "Hey, you guys, take five."

The two men who had been busy yanking off wallboard dropped their tools and took off their dust masks. On their way out, the younger man paused in the doorway.

"Hey, boss, almost forgot. Hayley called. She wants you to pick up bread and hamburger buns on your way home."

"Thanks, Sandy." Brodie chuckled. "Hen—"

"'Henpecked, that's what I am!'" the two workmen chanted together as if it was a story they'd heard many times before. And guffawing, they walked outside.

Brodie chuckled. "No respect," he said to Kendra. "I get no respect around here. One of these days…"

Kendra forced a small laugh but her mind was not

on what Brodie was saying, but on what Sandy had said.

Hayley. The name didn't ring a bell. She recalled no Hayley in high school. Where had Brodie met her, then? Had she been a summer visitor? One of those flashy city girls who came up to Lakeview for the holidays and dazzled the local boys at the Friday night dances?

"Over here," Brodie said.

She walked over to join him. He was wielding a heavy screwdriver.

"Watch this," he said.

He jabbed the screwdriver into one of the studs that had been revealed when the wallboard had been pulled off. The stud crumbled in a cloud of dust.

"Dry rot," he said.

"Is it bad?"

"It's bad. I've checked and it's spread all along this corner of the house. The kitchen, the mudroom, the kitchenette. We're looking at major reconstruction here."

"Oh, that's just *great!*" Kendra chewed her lip. "You're going to be working in both kitchens?"

"Yup."

She rubbed her hands down her arms, which suddenly felt chilly despite the warmth of the day. "How long will the job take?"

"Could be several weeks all told."

"We should move out."

He leaned back against the sink. "Yeah, it would be easier all round. Usually is, when renovations are major."

She murmured a sound of frustration and said, almost to herself, "I hate to uproot Megan again...just when we're getting settled."

"Yeah, it's hard on kids. Moving. D'you want to put the job on hold till you find some place to stay?"

"Yes, that would be best."

"Well, I guess we can knock off now," he said. "But listen...anything I can do to help out, just let me know."

Kendra wondered if she had ever met a more disconcerting man. A few minutes ago he'd been needling her, driving her crazy; now he was looking at her with concern in his eyes and offering her assistance.

"Thanks," she said. "That's kind of you. But I'm sure I'll manage. We'll probably end up renting a housekeeping suite in one of the motels at the school end of town—"

"Don't you think you'd be better off renting a house? Or even an apartment? Hell, Kendra, a motel's no place for a kid! As I said, we're looking at several weeks here."

"Thank you, Brodie. I'm well aware of that."

She hadn't meant to sound so chilly, but that's the way the words had come out and there was no taking them back.

"OK." He pushed himself from the counter. "So...give me a call when you're ready for us to get the job done."

He sauntered to the open doorway and braced a hand against the jamb as he looked out. "Hey, guys," he called, "come in and collect your gear. We're finished here for the time being."

Kendra slipped from the kitchen and hurried along the corridor to the sitting room.

She watched, from behind the curtains, till Brodie's red truck and the blue van had disappeared down the drive.

What rotten luck! she reflected. What was she going to do? Where would they go?

She'd have to discuss it with Megan after school.

But she knew that Megan would hate having to move, even though the move would just be temporary.

She wasn't looking forward to telling her the bad news.

"Do we have to talk *now,* Mom?"

"Yes," Kendra said. "Honey, something important has come up."

"OK. But then can we go to the rec center and sign me up for dance?"

They'd talked about it last night and Kendra had agreed that Megan could take beginners' jazz as long as she kept up with her ballet, too. "Yes, of course. In fact, let's go along there first. Then we can talk."

They cycled together to the rec center, which backed onto the lake, and after locking their bikes on the bike stand, went inside.

When they came out again, Kendra said, "Let's go for a walk along the beach. It's such a nice afternoon."

The shore was deserted and as they strolled along the pale grainy sand, Kendra looked around her with pleasure.

Lakeview was a pretty little town and down here, by the lake itself, the scenery was stunningly beautiful. The turquoise water was clear as glass today, disturbed only by the occasional flip of a trout as it leaped to the surface. Beyond rose the mountains, their snowcapped peaks a serrated line that separated land from azure sky. Up there the air would be crisp and cold; down here it was soft and warm.

"Mom, what do you want to talk about?" Megan shaded her eyes from the sun as she squinted up at her mother.

Kendra told her about her conversation with Brodie, and finished off by saying, "He agreed we ought to move out till all the work's finished."

Megan's eyes filled with dismay. "Where can we go?"

"I'll find a housekeeping unit in a nice motel—"

"Mom, the motels here are gross! They're right on the main street and they're noisy and—" She broke off as something else occurred to her. "You said I could have Jodi over to visit. No way would I ask her to some crummy motel room!" Her jaw jutted out. "Well, that'll please you anyway, since you don't want her to be my friend!"

"I didn't say that—"

"Well, she's still my friend. And since I can't ask her over on Saturday, then I'll just have to go to her place on Saturday."

"I don't want to fight with you over this, Megan."

"You started it!" Indignantly, Megan glared at her.

"I think what we both need now is dinner. Then after you've done your homework we can talk about it again."

"Homework!" Megan grimaced. "Uh-oh, I'm in big trouble."

"What is it?"

"The teacher didn't have my new math book yet, so she told me to borrow Jodi's and do the extra math at recess. I was supposed to give it back to Jodi later."

"And you forgot."

"It's here, in my backpack." Megan's face brightened. "We can drop it off on the way home, right?"

"I suppose we'll have to." Even as she spoke, Kendra reflected that the last place she wanted to go was anywhere near Brodie Spencer's place. If he saw her, he'd probably assume she was spying on him! But she didn't want Megan wandering about the town on her own. "Where do they live?"

"Right at the end of Calder Street. Number 46. I know it's got a red-tiled roof, and a white picket fence all around. Jodi told me all about it.'

So Brodie hadn't built himself a fancy house up in the new subdivision. Calder Street was in an older-established part of town. An area of modest homes.

"I know where Calder Street is. Let's go back then, and get our bikes."

Brodie had just mown the front lawn and was raking the cuttings when he sensed somebody was watching him.

He turned and looked up the street.

And saw Kendra Westmore.

She was standing, leaning on a bike, about three houses away, by the edge of the curb. And a little girl he'd never seen before was cycling up his drive.

A girl who was the image of her mother.

What was the kid's name again?

Megan.

He glanced back toward Megan's mother. She was gazing around with an *appearance* of nonchalance but he was pretty sure she hadn't expected to see him. And was no doubt more than a little embarrassed at having been spotted herself.

Megan wheeled to a halt and dropped her bike on the drive.

"Mr. Spencer?"

"That's me!"

She swung off her backpack and, delving into it, extricated a hardcover school textbook.

She walked over to him. "I'm Megan Westmore."

"Hi, Megan. Pleased to meet you. What can I do for you?"

"This is Jodi's math book. She'll need it for her homework tonight. Could you make sure she gets it?"

"Hey, in case I forget, why don't you give it to her yourself? She's 'round back in the pool. Go through that white picket gate, follow the path."

"Thanks, Mr. Spencer." She turned to the street and yelled, "Be right back, Mom!" And then she took off.

Her mother was still standing in the same spot, looking as if she'd rather be anywhere than where she was.

He gestured to her to come on up.

Even from the distance he could see her compress her lips. But two women passing by with their dogs were staring at her, and she walked toward him, pushing her bike.

He propped his rake against the mower and strolled across the lawn to meet her.

"Since you're here," he said, "why don't you come in and have a glass of something cold?"

"No, thanks," she said primly. "I need to get home."

"Oh, come on. Give the kids a break. What's your hurry? Here, let me have your bike."

For a moment, she kept her fingers rigidly around

the handgrips. Then she sighed. ''Just for a minute then.''

He set the bike on the grass and led her toward the picket gate. They walked around to the back together, and were just in time to see Megan and Jodi go into the house.

Hayley was alone in the pool, swimming laps.

''Hey, Hayley!'' he called.

She rolled over onto her back, and spreading her arms out to support her as she floated, gave him her attention.

She obviously hadn't expected to see anyone with him.

She blinked and then her gaze ran swiftly over their visitor. He saw a flash of something in her eyes, some indecipherable emotion—and then her expression closed up. Totally closed up. As if she wanted to hide what she was thinking. Inscrutable. That was the word to describe her.

What the hell was going on? Hayley was usually so open. Women! he thought. He'd never understand them!

''Come on out, honey,'' he said. ''There's somebody here I want you to meet.''

CHAPTER FOUR

CHILD BRIDE.

The words had popped into Kendra's head the moment she saw the other woman. Brodie must have stolen her out of the cradle, for Pete's sake—she still looked like a teenager! But as for her own earlier cynical assumption that Brodie had been trapped into marriage—if indeed he *had* been, he would have surely considered himself one very lucky man…

His wife was breathtakingly lovely, with a heart-shaped face, high cheekbones, enormous cornflower blue eyes, and fabulous brown hair…

And she'd had three children?

Unbelievable with that figure! She was climbing with effortless grace from the pool and Kendra could see not one silver stretch mark to mar her tanned skin, nor the faintest thickening of the teensy waist. And her breasts, though small, were as firm and perky as a seventeen-year-old's!

The "child bride" flicked back her sodden hair, and gathering up a towel, slung it around her neck and crossed to join them.

Kendra felt Brodie's fingertips lightly touch her back. "Kendra, this is Hayley. Hayley, this is Ms. Westmore. You've heard Jodi talk about her. Megan's mother."

"Hi, Ms. Westmore. Nice to meet you." Hayley's smile was reserved but her gaze seemed oddly assessing, as if she was summing Kendra up for some reason known only to herself.

And there was an edge of brittle tension about her that puzzled Kendra. She wondered if Brodie had noticed it. Were his wife's nerves strained because he'd brought a woman around? Was it something he did often?

"Let's go inside," Brodie said. "Meet the rest of the gang."

Feeling awkward, Kendra allowed herself to be ushered across the patio. To one side was a barbecue; the coals were not yet white-hot, but soon would be.

Brodie slid open the patio doors and they all trooped into a large airy kitchen.

A dark-haired boy of about twelve stood at the table, molding ground beef into hamburgers. He looked Kendra over, but kept on with what he was doing.

"Jack, this is Megan's mother. Ms. Westmore."

Jack grinned. "Yo. Can't shake hands unless you want to get covered in beef!"

"Hi, Jack," Kendra said. And wondered who he was.

"This is my boy Jack," Brodie said casually. "His turn to make dinner tonight. Enough there for two more people, son...if we spin it out a bit?"

"Sure, Dad."

"Hayley—" Brodie gestured toward the cupboard behind him "— could you get the oats for your brother and toss another handful in? Thanks."

Hayley flashed Kendra a smile. A bright smile, but she still seemed...uptight. "You'll stay? Nothing fancy, and just ice cream and brownies for dessert."

Kendra felt as if her mind had turned into a kaleidoscope and her thoughts had just been tossed out of order. She could make no sense of anything. She stared at Hayley who had already got out the package of oats. And at Jack, who had dumped the burgers back in the bowl, and—

"Earth to Westmore." Brodie passed a hand before her eyes. "You look…stunned. What's wrong?"

"I'm sorry." Her cheeks were warm. "I thought…" Oh, lord, how foolish she was! She'd jumped to all the wrong conclusions. She was an idiot of the first degree. She shrugged embarrassedly. "Nothing, really…"

Brodie persisted. "Thought…what?"

She decided to come clean.

She grimaced. "When Sandy said this morning that Hayley had called—I assumed she was your wife."

"Good grief!" Brodie chuckled. "My wife? Heck, no—though I must admit she has the henpecking off to a fine art—"

"But she can't be your daughter!" Kendra burst out, and she knew her protest sounded petulant.

Jack gave a splutter of laughter.

"Hayley," Brodie said, and there was still more than a hint of amusement in his voice, "would you set another couple of places on the picnic table, and I'll take Ms. Westmore through to the family room and give her a drink? I think she needs one after the shock she's just had. And it seems I have a bit of explaining to do."

Kendra shook her head. "Brodie, thank you for inviting us to stay but—"

He grasped her wrist and pulled her to the door.

She had the feeling that if she struggled, he'd just sweep her off her feet and carry her.

Besides, she did want to hear his explanation! The whole bewildering setup intrigued and fascinated her.

He led her across a hall floored with well-worn pale oak parquet. She stepped over tennis racquets, hockey sticks, runners, backpacks, and finally a large black Labrador. He was sound asleep—and snoring reverberatingly—on a rug in the open doorway of what was apparently the family room.

"Fetch," Brodie said.

"What?" Kendra looked around, confused.

He grinned. "The dog. That's his name."

"Oh." She laughed, and he paused. His fingers were still around her wrist; they felt like a comfortable bracelet.

"You should do that more often," he said softly.

"What?" Startled, she looked up into his eyes.

"Laugh."

Their eyes locked...and remained locked. His fingers tightened around her wrist. They no longer felt comfortable; they felt...disturbing. The pad of his thumb pressed on her pulse; the contact was intimate. Dizzying.

Kendra had the odd sensation that their surroundings had disappeared; that the rest of the world had disappeared. The teasing warmth in Brodie's eyes enfolded her, like a cashmere blanket on a chilly night. She wanted to cuddle up to him, slide her arms around him—

She shivered.

He blinked. And the spell was broken.

"You promised me a drink!" she said briskly, sliding her wrist free.

He ushered her forward. "What'll you have? Beer, sherry, wine—I have a nice dry Riesling—"

"The Riesling, thanks. That would be lovely."

He crossed to the bar area set in an alcove, and while he poured the drinks, she took the opportunity to look around.

The room was rectangular in shape, with a bay window overlooking the back garden and pool. The carpet was a practical mud color, the armchairs and couches shabby but inviting-looking. Bookcases lined one wall. Most of the adjacent wall was taken up by a floor-to-ceiling brick fireplace with built-in shelves on either side. On one shelf was arranged an assortment of trophies—for skating, ballet, and ice hockey; on another sat stereo equipment; and on a third a 27-inch TV set flanked by precarious piles of videos. The oak coffee table in the center of the room was massive, its surface littered with newspapers, teen magazines, Barbies, hockey cards, a half-finished jigsaw, an opened package of chocolate chip cookies, a pack of cards...

Something ached, deep in Kendra's heart.

This was a real home, she thought wistfully. Not impressive or grand like Rosemount; but the kind of place a child would hurry home to after school, the kind of place a man could relax in after a hard day's work.

She turned and Brodie was standing beside her.

She took the wineglass, held it by the stem.

"It's a bit of a mess," he said. "I could tell you you'd caught us on a bad day, but heck, that would be a downright lie!" His eyes twinkled. "It's pretty damned tidy right now, compared with the way it'll be by the time Friday rolls around. Saturday morning's housecleaning time in the Spencer house. We all pitch in right after breakfast, and nobody gets to leave till it's done.''

''Brodie—''

He gestured toward one of the sofas. ''Sit down.''

She sat, and the low-slung sofa with its squashy cushions was even more comfortable than its looks promised.

Brodie took the armchair opposite her. He leaned forward, his beer mug cupped in his hands, and rested his forearms on his thighs.

''They're my brother's kids,'' he said. And the twinkle had gone from his eyes. ''Jack's. Maureen's. They died in an accident six years ago, along with my father—''

''Blue told me about the accident.'' Kendra felt the smarting of tears and willed them away. ''I didn't know, Brodie. I didn't even know you had a brother. And Blue didn't mention the children. So when you dropped Jodi off at the school on Monday and I heard her call you Dad, I just assumed...''

''The younger two call me Dad. It seemed natural after the first while. Specially for Jodi. She was only two. Jack, he was six. Hayley...well, it was different for Hayley. She was eleven, going on twelve. She's never forgotten her parents. When she calls me anything,'' he added, his voice holding the very faintest tinge of regret, ''it's just...Brodie.''

For a long moment there was silence between them. From the other end of the house, they heard Jack's voice calling to somebody.

After a while, Kendra said, ''So...you took them all on after...Jack and his wife died, and your father was gone. There was just you? Nobody else?''

''Just me. Maureen had no folks.''

Kendra wondered if she'd ever been so wrong about anybody.

"Brodie..." Over the lump in her throat, his name came out in a choked sort of way. The tears she'd tried to keep at bay started to brim over.

"Hell, Kendra, I didn't mean to make you cry!" He put down his beer glass and got to his feet. "That's the last thing I want!"

He was halfway over to her, an odd light burning in his eyes, when the door burst open. Swiftly, Kendra swiped away her tears with her fingertips and swallowed back the lump in her throat.

"Dad!" Jodi burst into the room, with Megan right behind her, leaping over Fetch, her face bright with joy. "Is Megan really staying for the barbecue?"

She ran to Brodie and slid to a stop beside him. Megan hung back, but her eyes gleamed as they met her mother's.

"Yeah, poppet, Megan's staying, and her mom is, too."

"Well, Jack says to come now, the burgers'll be ready in a minute."

The moment had passed. Whatever might have happened had the children not interrupted, Kendra didn't know.

But as Brodie escorted them all out to the backyard, she realized the timing couldn't have been better.

She'd been so moved by the sacrifice Brodie had made—a sacrifice that he didn't seem to recognize as such—that she might have done something stupid.

Like let him kiss her.

Which was what she thought he'd been going to do.

* * *

Brodie shifted restlessly on the cushioned chaise, an after-dinner coffee on the cedar patio table by his side, as he watched Kendra stroll down the back lawn with Hayley.

Bitterness coiled through him. Bitterness he tried to suppress. Hell, he'd sworn he'd never let himself think about the past again; had made himself that solemn promise on Christmas Eve, eight years ago, after Kendra Westmore had snubbed him so royally.

He'd gone down to the Hoedown Bar later that night and had gotten drunker than he'd ever been, before or since. And he'd sworn before God that he'd never waste another moment thinking about the snooty bitch!

It had been hard, but he'd managed; and the fact that she'd never set foot in Lakeview again had made it easier.

But now she was back in his life.

And she was *still* denying him.

Denying everything that had happened between them.

Denying it by her silence.

Well, he'd die before he'd be the one to bring it up. He had his pride, after all—and maybe it was the only thing he had going for him, as far as she was concerned. The only thing that kept him from making a damned fool of himself.

Again.

The landscape seemed suddenly blurred.

He was obsessed with her; there was no getting away from it. And he had been, from the first time he'd seen her—seen her, that was, as anything but a kid. He'd been digging one of the Rosemount flower beds when she'd come out the front door, wearing a pink dress, her hair a dazzle of white gold. To him she had looked like a fairy princess.

But she'd always been out of his reach...

Till that night in Seattle.

He blinked and his vision cleared.

The sun was low in the sky now, causing shadows to whisper over the sprawling garden. In its mellow rays, her hair glowed like pale fire.

He felt a twist in his groin.

That hair, that pale silky hair, with a texture so smooth, so light, it had sifted through his fingers like the moonbeams that had blessed them as they made love; made love with the sound of "Yesterday's Memories" drifting to them in the hot September night—

No, not made love.

At the time, he'd believed they'd made love. He had made love. Tender passionate caring love. Protected love.

She had had sex.

And later...had walked.

His gut knotted. This time, it would be different.

This time he would be in control. If she ever gave in to this sexual attraction that still simmered between them, he would be the one to walk afterward.

Then maybe his obsession with her would fade.

Leave him forever.

And give him the peace he so desperately craved.

"Are you planning to stay in Lakeview permanently?"

Kendra paused as Hayley asked her the question. "Yes. I've always loved this town. I want to bring Megan up here."

How odd it was, Kendra mused, that Hayley was so different when the two of them were alone.

Over dinner, the teenager had been reticent; but as soon as the two of them had come down here, leaving Brodie on the patio, she had changed. She was warm, natural, friendly. It was almost as if she hadn't wanted Brodie to know she liked his guest. But why?

"Jodi said you're a widow. I'm sorry."

Kendra felt a twinge of guilt. She didn't always, when faced with her lie, because in her own mind it was a very necessary lie...but somehow, with this frank-faced teenager, she was uncomfortable with the dishonesty. "I've been on my own, with Megan, for six years now. I'm getting on with my life, Hayley. I don't look back, but forward."

"So you think you'll marry again, some day?"

There, the tension had returned to her voice. Was she afraid that she, Kendra, had designs on Brodie? That was a laugh!

"It's not on my agenda at the moment. I'm not ruling it out...but marrying again is...unlikely."

And that was because it was unlikely she'd ever find a man she could trust enough to tell him the truth about Megan.

With practised skill she shut out the dark memories that tried to gate-crash her mind...but she could do nothing about the shiver that rippled through her.

"Are you cold?" Hayley's tone was concerned. "Can I get you a sweater?"

"Thanks." She managed a smile. "But I really have to get Megan home now. We've surely overstayed our welcome."

"Oh, no, not at all!" Hayley hesitated and then went on, in a rush. "Ms. Westmore—"

"Why don't you call me Kendra? I'm only a few years older than you."

"You don't mind?"

"Heavens no!"

"OK, Kendra, then." Hayley toyed with a strand of the long brown hair that tasseled over her shoulders. "About Saturday...would you please join us?"

Kendra felt like a worm as she met Hayley's clear blue eyes. "I've told Megan she must wait till Friday before—"

"I know." A small frown tugged Hayley's eyebrows together. "Ms. Westmore...Kendra...Jodi's a gregarious child—and very popular with her schoolmates. She's got loads of friends, but she's never wanted to have one special friend...till now. Those two—well you saw them over dinner. You'd think they'd known each other forever."

Kendra heard a scraping sound and as she glanced at the patio, she saw Brodie had got up from his chaise.

The sun gilded his lean body as he stood watching them; and she felt a now-familiar pull of attraction for this man who was not the man she'd believed him to be.

He was so much more.

But of course she had never really known him before. He'd been wild and bad and reckless with a reputation that would have made Don Juan look like a monk. How was she to know that under that tough exterior had beaten a heart that was softer than a melted marshmallow?

A man of honor and integrity and compassion.

Hayley said to her, quietly, "Will you come, on Saturday...for the kids?"

Brodie had started strolling toward them. Oh, that sexy way he walked, it really got to her! She felt her pulse quicken; her breasts tighten. She needed to get out of there—fast!

She turned back to Hayley. "I'm afraid I'm going to be really busy all this week. I have to look for a motel unit and then pack all the stuff Megan and I will need, and cart it there. But thanks so much for the invitation. I'll accept now, for Megan. I know the girls will have fun."

Brodie had reached them. And heard the last of the conversation.

"You won't join us?" His eyes were veiled, as if he'd been thinking very private thoughts that still lingered; thoughts he wanted to keep to himself.

"I'm going to be busy," she said. "Maybe some other time."

"I'll pick Megan up. Around two?"

"That's all right," she said, her voice coming out much more stiffly than she'd meant it to. "I'll drop her off."

"OK, great. Let's go inside now, and see what those two youngsters are up to."

Hayley said she'd stay outside for a while, so Kendra and Brodie went back into the house alone.

Megan and Jodi weren't in the kitchen.

"They're probably up in Jodi's room," Brodie said. "Come on through to the hall—you can go out the front way."

Once in the foyer, he excused himself.

"Be back in a sec," he said, and bounded up the stairs.

Left to her own devices, Kendra looked casually around and observed that every wall was adorned with framed photographs. Family snaps, for the most part. One picture in particular drew her attention. It hung above the phone table, and was the biggest of all.

She stepped over to study it.

It was a family portrait—a studio portrait, in colour, and framed in a plain gold frame. She had no difficulty guessing who the five people were:

Jack, Maureen, and their three children.

Jack looked very like Brodie—same black wavy hair, same lean attractive face, same blue-green eyes. He was heavier-set, though; and more stolid-looking. His wife was very pretty, with Hayley's cornflower blue eyes and brown hair. Jodi was on her father's lap, and must have been about a year old when the picture was taken. She was plump and smiling and had the look of a child finding it hard to sit still. Jack Junior and Hayley were easily recognizable; Jack's grin was broad; Hayley's expression sweetly shy.

Kendra sighed. A year later, that family had been shattered apart, never to be the same again.

She turned away, feeling a heaviness in her heart that hadn't been there before—but again, filled with admiration for Brodie...no, more than admiration. Intense respect and absolute awe. He had brought up a family to be proud of.

She tensed as she heard him run down the stairs.

Turning, she looked up at him.

"They'll be down in a minute," he said. Mouth tilted wryly, he added, "Never saw two kids getting on like that before. It's uncanny—they're like two halves of the same coin. Heck, they've only known each other a couple of days and they're already finishing each other's sentences!"

He reached the foot of the stairs and was so close

she could smell his distinctive male scent. She wanted to step back, away from him. But held her ground.

"I've enjoyed my visit, Brodie," she said. "You've created a wonderful...ambience in this house—"

"I created nothing, Kendra. This was Jack and Maureen's house. Whatever magic's here, they created it. I just moved in...after the accident. And I've tried to keep things exactly as they were, for the sake of the kids. I've been thinking lately, though, that it's time to make a change. This place is too small, we need room to spread..."

"Would you build?"

"Probably."

"You've done very well, Brodie." Kendra leaned against the newel post and looked at him quizzically. "Your business...it's a great success."

"You're wondering how I got started?"

"I'm curious, yes."

"Pops had a big life insurance policy. My brother and I were joint beneficiaries. The way the policy was written, if either Jack or I died before Pops, the surviving brother would get all. So...it came to me. And just at that time, Lakeview Construction came up for sale. So I bought it. The kids have a half share in the business—what they want to do with it they can decide when they're older."

"It was always a good going concern...but on a much smaller scale. It's incredible what you've done with it. Your father would be proud of you—of what you've achieved."

"Yeah, he would—though he wasn't an ambitious man himself. I still have the old shack, by the way." He was looking at her now in a different way; with a hint of...challenge? Or was it once again that mockery? "On the wrong side of the tracks. Where Pops brought Jack and me up. I held on to it—"

Kendra hadn't been aware of Megan and Jodi running down the stairs till she heard Jodi pipe up, "He goes over there, sometimes, when we're all too much for him—right, Dad?" She grinned. "It's his escape from bedlam. That's what he calls it, Ms. Westmore!"

Kendra was glad of the interruption. She didn't like it when Brodie talked to her in that mocking way; she hadn't chosen to be born into a wealthy family. And she'd been about to tell him just that. Which no doubt would have started them in on another unpleasant argument—something she wanted to avoid.

"Yeah, and the older you get, Miss Smartypants, the oftener I feel the need to escape!" Brodie swatted out at Jodi's bottom, but with a giggle she skipped out of reach. "OK, Megan, you ready to leave this madhouse?"

"It's not a madhouse, Mr. Spencer. It's the nicest house I've ever been in," Megan said, sincerity ringing in her voice. "And I'm glad Mom's letting me come back on Saturday. I can't wait!"

That night, as Kendra tucked Megan into bed, Megan said, "What's a matchmaker, Mom?"

"A matchmaker?" Kendra brushed back a strand of blond hair that had fallen over Megan's forehead. "It's a person who loves plotting to get other people married! Why?"

"Jodi told me that's what Hayley is. A matchmaker. She wants to get their dad married."

"Really?" Odd—hadn't she herself gotten the distinct impression that Hayley was *afraid* Brodie might find a wife?

''Mmm. She's been looking around for ages but hasn't found anybody suitable yet. She says she'll know her the minute she sees her. It'll have to be somebody really special, because their dad is so special. Hayley has to find somebody before next Fall, that's what Jodi heard Hayley tell her best friend Zoe. Hayley wants to go away to college next year but she won't go if her dad's still on his own. And,'' Megan paused for effect, ''what made Jodi feel really bad was, Hayley said it was because of her.''

''Because of Jodi?''

''Yup. 'Cos Jodi's going to be at an age when she's really gonna need a mom around. Well, Hayley isn't her mom, but she is, in a way. Know what I mean?''

Oh, dear. What a tangle. And obviously Brodie wasn't meant to know about any of this. ''Yes, I do. But Mr. Spencer may not ever want to marry!''

''Oh, he'll have to. Hayley said that to Zoe. She said he would have to marry eventually, 'cos men have needs.'' She quirked an eyebrow at her mother, and it was obvious she hadn't a clue what those needs were.

Kendra choked back a chuckle. ''Enough talk, young lady! What *you* need is a good night's rest!'' She got up and walked to the door. As she reached for the light switch, Megan said, in a different voice, a quieter voice, ''Mom, at the Spencer house they've got family pictures up everywhere. Even photos of Jodi's mom and real Dad, though they're dead. How come we don't have any pictures of my dad?''

Kendra froze. She'd been awaiting this moment for a long time; in fact she'd often wondered why it hadn't yet arisen. Was it because Megan was such an exceptionally sensitive child and had therefore sensed that the subject of her father was one her mother studiously avoided?

"Mom?" The child's eyes were puzzled. "You don't even have any photos of your wedding day! How come?"

Kendra felt her heart sink. What could she say?

What would Megan think if she were told the truth?

There are no photos of the wedding day...because there never was a wedding!

With legs heavy as lead, she walked back to the bed.

"Honey," she said, "we'll talk about this when...you're older. Some things...well, you're just too young to understand. But I promise that one day I'll explain everything. Could you have patience, and...wait?"

"I feel like something's missing about me, Mom." Tears glistened in Megan's eyes. "Like I never did have a dad. Like it was just you and me...forever." Her voice caught on the last word, and Kendra felt as if her heart was breaking.

Megan wanted something she couldn't give.

At least, not now. Not yet. And perhaps...never.

Tears blurring her gaze, she sank onto the edge of the mattress and tried to pull her daughter into her arms.

But Megan twisted away with a sob.

And buried her face in her pillow.

CHAPTER FIVE

BRODIE poked his head around the office door at a quarter past five on Friday.

"I'm taking off now, Mitzi."

His office manager looked up from the papers on her desk. "So what's on the agenda tonight?"

"You need to ask?"

"I guess not! Georgio's gonna be glued to the set, too. Always is, in hockey season. Heck, I could strip naked and dance in front of him and he'd just say 'Move over, honey, you're blocking my view!'"

"A man after my own heart!" Brodie chuckled and was still smiling as he got into his truck and drove it around to the front exit.

He had to pause at the stop sign, and was just about to ease out into the traffic when he saw a familiar white Honda pull in at the Lakeview Motel car park across the street.

There were no vehicles behind him, so he waited, letting the truck idle.

Moments later, he saw Kendra emerge from her car. She made for the trunk. Flipping it up, she reached inside and hauled out a cumbersome cardboard box, and dumped it on the ground. Then she hauled out another smaller box.

She straightened, closed the trunk, and rubbed a hand over the small of her back as if it ached.

Brodie checked that the street was clear and then swung the truck across the four lanes and into the motel car park. Pulling up beside the Honda, he jumped down onto the tarmac.

"Hi, there," he said. "Need some help?"

Kendra glanced up, and he saw that her face was flushed and her skin moist with perspiration. The flush deepened as she looked at him.

"No, thanks. I can manage—"

"That was a rhetorical question." He hoisted up the larger box. "Come on. I'll take this inside for you." Over his shoulder he added as he rounded her car and made for the motel entrance, "You've taken a unit here?"

He thought he heard a sigh of exasperation. Then he heard her footsteps coming up fast behind him.

"I've taken a housekeeping unit," she said breathlessly as she caught up. "Just on a week-to-week basis, till I see how it's going to work out."

He stood back to let her go through the revolving doors ahead of him and stole the chance to feast his eyes on her. Her hair, today, was beautifully French-braided, and she was wearing a fuchsia muslin sundress with spaghetti straps, a narrow belt, and a long, seductively clingy skirt.

She looked fragile and feminine and sexy as hell.

And he wanted to drag her into his arms and kiss her till she moaned. He tightened his grip on the cardboard box and the corner jabbed sharply into his groin.

The stab of pain had the same effect as an icy shower.

For which he should be thankful; the last thing he needed was for Kendra Westmore to know that the very sight of her was enough to cause him grave discomfort!

Her unit was on the main floor, and he followed her along the corridor, determinedly transferring his gaze from the tantalizing wiggle of her hips to the insipid paintings adorning the walls.

She set her box on the floor outside her door and rummaged in her purse for the key. When she pushed the door open, he could see past her to the sitting room windows and beyond the windows to the sprawling buildings of his own company, with its flashing neon Lakeview Construction sign.

She crossed the short hall into the sitting room and dumped her box on a couch. He set his on the floor beside the TV.

"Thanks," she said, rotating her shoulders. "I've spent the day carting boxes over here and my arms feel as if they're going to drop out of their sockets!"

He looked around. "You've packed everything away already."

"Yes, now I've only got these two boxes to see to. One's groceries and the one you carried in is mainly Megan's books and some of her toys."

He moved around the unit, glancing casually into a pastel-pink bedroom, a small bathroom, a galley kitchen. He opened a door in the hall and found a closet.

"Just the one bedroom?" He stepped back into the sitting room.

"That's a Hide-a-bed." She indicated a sofa by the window. "Megan can have the bedroom. That way, I won't disturb her if I'm moving around after she's asleep."

"It's pretty cramped."

"The place we had in Vancouver was no bigger."

"Then that must have been *really* cramped...with the three of you."

"The three of us?"

"Your husband. When he was alive."

He felt the tension click into place. From open and casual, she switched—in a snap!—to closed and uptight. She walked to the window and stood looking out. "Megan and I moved there after his death. It was only the two of us."

Because she was wearing the strappy sundress, he could see the taut pull of the muscles in her back and shoulders.

"And before that?" he said. "Where did you live?"

"Seattle. That's where Megan was born."

"What did he do, your husband?"

She turned round and met his gaze steadily. "Brodie, do you mind if we don't talk about him? I still find it...difficult."

After six years? He itched to know why. Was she still in love with the man? "Sorry." He moved toward her. "I didn't mean to upset you."

"You didn't. It's just that I...prefer...not to talk about the past." She wrapped her arms around herself, defensively. And as she did, her left spaghetti strap slid down over her shoulder.

Before she could move he'd reached out and tucked the tip of his index finger under the tiny rolled strap. He heard her breath catch. But he took his sweet time sliding the strap back into place, savoring every deliciously tantalizing second. Her skin was warm, sunbrowned and smooth. Her scent was heaven. Her closeness hell.

Her gaze had skittered to his with a wide and wary

expression that said "What are you going to do next?"

What he wanted to do next was unbraid her hair and let it spill out luxuriantly so he could bury his face in it.

What he did instead was tell himself that the time wasn't right to start something that once started, there would be no stopping. But heck, who wanted to stop?

He ran a fingertip lightly along her collarbone. "So...where's Megan."

"Megan?" Her eyes had become glazed.

"Megan. Where is she?"

"Oh." Her lashes flickered. She blinked several times. And gulped. "Megan. She's...at her jazz lesson. I have to pick her up in ten minutes."

He dropped his hand, and he could have sworn he saw a shadow cross her eyes. A shadow of... disappointment?

Which was nothing compared to how he felt.

He suppressed a groan and glanced at his watch. With a melodramatic double take, he said, "Hey, I'd better be on my way, too! It's my night to make dinner. I've promised the kids pizza and I need to get the kitchen all cleaned up afterward, before the big game."

"Hockey?"

"An exhibition game on TV. The Canucks and the New York Islanders." He forced his legs to walk him to the door. "I'll see you tomorrow," he said as he opened it. "When you drop Megan off."

"Right," she said. "See you tomorrow. And thanks again for your help."

"You're welcome," he said. "It was my pleasure."

And *that* was the understatement of the year!

The motel dining room had been recently painted, and the smell of paint lingered. The tables were covered in shell-pink cloths, and in the center of each one was a fluted white vase with a spray of plastic freesias.

As Kendra and Megan took their seats, Kendra said, "We won't be eating here again, sweetie. It's just that I didn't feel like cooking tonight...I've been on the go all day and I thought this would be a treat."

Megan spread her serviette over her lap. "Mom, can we go see that Walt Disney movie tonight? It starts at seven."

Megan had seemed subdued since the night she'd been refused answers to her questions about her father. Guilt had been gnawing away at Kendra over it; now she felt the least she could do was accede to this small request.

"Sure," she said. "In which case, we'd better hurry up and order!"

They did, and after they'd finished their meal, they walked quickly along to their unit.

"The cinema will be air-conditioned," she called to Megan who'd scooted into the bathroom. "We'd better change into something warm."

She'd packed her own clothes in the bedroom dresser and after slipping off her sundress, put on a sweatshirt and jeans.

Megan came into the bedroom and Kendra took her turn in the bathroom. When she came out, she found Megan waiting in the hall, her hand on the door to the lobby. She'd changed into jeans and had slung a fleecy cardigan over her T-shirt.

"We'd better hurry, Mom. It's quarter to seven."

Kendra picked up her purse. "Let's just hope there's not one huge queue!"

Brodie swiped the green-and-white checked dishcloth over the countertop, draped it over the tap, flicked on the dishwasher and made for the fridge.

He opened it and took out a beer.

The can was icy-cold; he licked his lips in anticipation. The game wasn't due to start for a while, but he was looking forward to relaxing in his leather recliner—and having the house to himself for a couple of hours.

Jack was next door at his buddy's; and Hayley was taking Jodi to some Walt Disney movie. She'd promised Jodi ages ago, and this was the very last night it was showing.

He popped open the beer can and took a slurp. Man, did that *ever* taste good! He'd had a helluva busy day, been on the go constantly from seven till five; he couldn't *wait* to get his feet up and—

Jodi burst into the kitchen but when she saw him, she turned and ran out again. But not before he'd seen that she was crying.

He muttered under his breath.

And putting down his beer, took off after her.

He caught her at the foot of the stairs.

"OK," he said, and held her firmly by the shoulders. "Tell me what's wrong."

"It's...Hayley." Tears the size of marbles rolled down her cheeks. "She can't take me to the movie."

"What the..." He felt a surge of anger. A promise was a promise. "Where is she?"

"She's up in her room—"

"You stay right here, young lady!" He thundered up the stairs. "I'll be—"

"But, Dad, you don't understand!" she called after him.

What was there to understand! He strode along the corridor, hammered on Hayley's door, and almost before he heard her faint, "Come in", he barged into the bedroom.

She was lying curled up on the bed and her face was gray. Gray as old ashes. And her eyes were shadowed. With…pain?

"Hayley?" Slowly, he walked over the carpet. "What's up, sweetie?"

"I'm sorry." Her voice shook. "I…I can't go out. Not tonight."

"But what's the matter?"

She looked at him, with a pleading expression in her eyes, the way an animal might look when it wanted to explain but didn't have the words.

He heard a sound behind him.

He turned. And frowned as he saw Jodi standing in the doorway, her lips trembling, her face tear-stained.

She walked over to him and gestured for him to bend down.

He did. And raising herself on her tiptoes, she pressed her mouth to his ear.

"It's PMS, Dad." Her whisper quavered. "Whatever that is, but Hayley said she can't talk about it to you. 'Cos you're a man."

He straightened and stared bewilderedly at Hayley.

PMS? What the hell was that!

Ah. The penny dropped. He felt a dull color seep into his face.

"Sweetie," he said to Hayley, "is there anything I can do to help?"

"Could you fill this?" She uncurled slightly and he saw she had a rubber hot water bottle pressed against her stomach. She held it out to him. "From the tap will do. I've taken painkillers, they should work soon."

He went into her en suite, ran the tap till the water was piping hot, and refilled the bottle.

When he came out again, Jodi had disappeared and Hayley was huddled under her duvet.

He gave her the bottle. "Ok, honey?"

Her cheeks had taken on a pink flush; an embarrassed flush. "Thanks." She lifted the duvet, tucked the bottle in place and curled up tightly again.

He felt so damned useless. What did he know about women's woes? Nothing! This could have been going on for years—probably had been going on for years—and he hadn't known a damn thing about it!

Poor kid, how she must have missed—still must miss—having a mother to talk things over with...

"What are we going to do?" Hayley's voice seemed to come from far away. "About Jodi...and the movie? I hate having to let her down. If there was only someone else to take her..."

Hayley's lashes fluttered, he realized she was becoming drowsy. Whatever pills she'd used were taking effect.

"Don't you worry about that," he said softly. "You just rest, and try to feel better."

He made no sound as he crossed the bedroom, no sound as he closed the door behind him.

Thoughts tumbling over each other, he walked back along the corridor, and down the stairs.

He crossed the foyer. Came to the open doorway of the family room. The TV was on. His steps faltered.

He stood there, looking at the set.

Yearningly.

He told himself not to be such a selfish clod.

And went to look for his younger daughter.

"Megan, wait up!"

Kendra and Megan were hurrying across the carpeted foyer toward Cinema 3 when the shrill voice called after them.

They both turned, and Kendra saw Jodi running toward them. The foyer was now deserted, except for themselves and an usher. The movie was due to start in exactly one minute.

When Jodi caught up with them, she panted, "Can we sit together? Please, Ms. Westmore?"

"Of course," Kendra said. But it surprised her that the child would be allowed to go to a movie alone—even in a little town like Lakeview, where the crime rate was almost nonexistent. "And you can have my popcorn. The concession stand's closed up already—"

"Mom, I'll share mine with Jodi, OK?"

"If that's what you want." She put a hand on Megan's shoulder and turned her toward the open doorway to the cinema. The usher had already started to close the doors.

"Only a few seats left," he said. "Halfway down. Right-hand aisle."

He guided them down the aisle, shining his flashlight onto the sloping floor, and escorted them to the empty seats. There were four, the last vacant seats in the small theater, and they were directly next to the aisle.

Jodi eased in first and scrambled right over. Megan followed suit, and then Kendra sat beside Megan.

That left the aisle seat, next to Kendra, empty.

Good. She could stretch out, make herself comfortable.

It had been a rush to get to the movie theater. They'd walked but Kendra had misjudged the distance, and they'd ended up last in a long queue.

Lucky to get seats, she mused. And dropped a cluster of popcorn into her mouth. Mmm. It was ages since she'd been to a movie. This wasn't her choice, but still, it might be fun—

Somebody...a man...lowered himself into the empty seat next to her.

He moved around a bit, seemed to find it hard to get comfortable. In the end, she noticed from the corner of her eye, he slid his long legs out into the aisle.

He wasn't really sitting. He was...sprawling. And he was taking up *way* too much space. In fact, he was crowding into hers. Her initial mild irritation changed swiftly to intense revulsion as his muscular upper arm pressed intimately against her shoulder. She could feel the warmth of his flesh, for heaven's sake, through her sweatshirt! She could even smell the hint of beer on his breath!

What kind of a man came, on his own, to a kids' movie?

She stiffened, and pointedly leaned well away from him. Now she was pressing into Megan. Megan murmured in protest.

And then...

Then, the disgusting man helped himself to her popcorn!

With a gasp of shock, she swiveled in her seat to give him a piece of her mind.

But at that second, the movie blasted into the opening scene and the reflected light from the screen illuminated his face. Even as words of outrage and contempt raced to her lips, she became aware of two things at the same time.

The man in the next seat was laughing at her.

And he was no stranger.

"Relax, honey!" He grinned as he slid an arm over the back of her seat. "It's only me."

Brodie had dropped Jodi off at the cinema doors.

"Here's the money, you get the tickets while I park. Get yourself inside so you don't miss the start of the movie, and I'll find you."

He'd found her all right...but he'd almost choked when he'd recognized the blond sitting a couple of seats along.

Well, I'll be! he'd thought. And decided to have a bit of fun. Which indeed he'd had!

But now, with his arm stretched—casually but deliberately—over the back of her seat, he was getting more than he'd bargained for. She was wearing perfume that made him think of summer meadows sprinkled with wildflowers. Wildflowers tangled in silky blond hair. Silky blond hair fanned out in seductive invitation over naked tanned shoulders and gloriously rich breasts, while his hands—

He cleared his throat and shifted awkwardly as his jeans seemed to shrink at the stress point over his crotch. This was no place to be having erotic fantasies—squashed into a narrow seat and surrounded by innocent kids!

He gritted his teeth and stared at the screen.

Concentrate! he told himself. Blot her out of your mind and concentrate on the damned movie!

Rain was spitting down when they came out of the theater.

Kendra felt a stab of panic when Brodie, after discovering she and Megan didn't have the car, offered to drive them back to the motel.

She had no intention of prolonging the evening. The more she saw of the man, the more she was attracted to him. She'd been limp with disappointment that afternoon when he'd left the unit without kissing her—she'd been so sure he was going to do just that!

And hadn't she just spent the last two hours in the movie theater in a turmoil of desperate lust as every time he casually shifted his arm along the back of her seat she hoped/prayed/feared it would move to her shoulder and his fingertips would find/touch/caress her nipples?

Wanton hussy!

But even as she opened her mouth to refuse his offer, she saw that Jodi and Megan had scuttled away along the street and were already standing impatiently at Brodie's truck.

Nothing to do for it but to give in gracefully.

"Thanks," she said. "We'd appreciate that."

But she made sure the two children sat between them on the front seat of the truck.

And when they reached the motel, she said hurriedly, even before he'd pulled on the brake, "I'd ask you in for a coffee but it's past Megan's regular bedtime and I'm sure you want to get home and shoot Jodi off to bed, too."

"Can't they just come in for a minute?" Megan pleaded.

This from the kid who'd ranted that no way would she ever invite Jodi Spencer into any crummy motel room!

"Oh, I'd like that!" Jodi said. "Just for a minute, Ms. Westmore? We won't stay or be a nuisance, will we, Dad!"

Kendra held her breath.

"Honey, we'd better get home," Brodie said. "I want to check on Hayley."

Silently, Kendra expelled her breath. "Is something wrong?" She looked over the children's heads at Brodie.

"She wasn't feeling too well when we left." His gaze was on her hair; his eyes cloudy as if he was thinking of touching it. She could have sworn, in the movie theater, that he *had* run his fingertips over it, more than once.

Was her face as pink as it felt? "I'm sorry. I hope she'll be feeling better by the time you get home." She scooped up her purse from the cab floor and patted Megan's hand. "Let's go. Jodi can come in another time, OK?"

Brodie made to get out, but she quickly said, "Don't bother," and shoved open her door. The mood he was in, he might just drag her into his arms; and the mood she was in, she might not be able to resist. Sexual tension shimmered between them like a live thing! Even sitting here, she felt her legs weaken at the glassy expression in his eyes. She jumped down and her knees gave way under her. She managed to lock them, and catch Megan who'd jumped down after her.

"Night, Megan," Jodi called. "See you tomorrow."

Brodie looked over at Kendra and said, "How about changing your mind and joining us tomorrow afternoon? And don't tell me you're busy! You've only a couple of boxes to put away!"

"Thanks, but I have to go up to the house in the afternoon. I'm interviewing prospective gardeners."

"Ah." He revved up the engine. He was wearing a V-necked sweater with the sleeves shoved up and her gaze caught on his forearms as he tightened his grip on the steering wheel. Wonderful arms, strong and muscled, with a sprinkling of wiry black hair. Something inside her clenched, as she recalled again how it felt having one of those arms along the back of her seat all evening. So near…yet so far…

She slammed the door, and gave driver and passenger a wave.

She and Megan stood, sheltered under an awning, till the truck had driven out the exit and disappeared along the street.

Megan slid her hand into one of her mother's.

"That was such a fun night, Mom. Aren't you glad Jodi and her dad came, too?"

Kendra thought of Brodie's eyes, the way they'd caressed her—warm with promise—as she'd waved goodbye.

"Yes." A shivery feeling—not unpleasant—rippled down her spine. 'I was glad they came, too."

"And did you enjoy the movie?"

"Oh…oh, sure, it was fine."

She certainly wasn't about to admit to her daughter—or to anyone else—that not even for a million dollars could she have sketched out the film's story.

Her mind had been on other things!

Brodie looked in on Hayley as soon as he and Jodi got home. She was sound asleep; and her face had some color.

He crept out of the room and after getting Jodi off to bed, he went downstairs again.

Jack was just coming in the front door.

"Hi, Dad." He yawned. "I'm off to bed. See you tomorrow."

"Night, son." He put his arm around Jack's neck and gave him a brawny man-to-man hug. "Sleep tight."

Jack went upstairs and Brodie ambled through to the kitchen where he poured himself a tall glass of cold milk. He spotted a packet of chocolate bars on the counter; he helped himself to a couple.

Taking his snack through to the family room, he got settled in his leather recliner, clicked on the TV and waited to see the score.

It was 2-all.

He peeled the silver paper off the first chocolate bar, and munching the bar happily, he focused all his attention on the game.

The motel Hide-A-Bed was remarkably comfortable.

But Kendra was just drifting off to sleep when a sound outside in the parking lot disturbed her. She murmured, and shifted her position. Wished the noise would go away.

It didn't. A car was idling, perhaps the driver was dropping somebody off and they were chatting. His radio was on, and the music was drifting in through her open window.

"Yesterday's Memories."

Her pulse gave a ragged jerk and her throat went dry as she recognized the familiar melody.

It had been the theme song of the Black Bats Group—a rock group from Oregon whose meteoric rise to success had been front-page news everywhere they performed. Tragically they'd all been killed in a plane crash, five years ago...

But before then, she'd gone to their Seattle concert.

When she was seventeen.

Nine years ago this month.

And ever since, when she heard that particular song, she felt goose bumps rise all over her body.

Just as they were rising now.

She moaned, and hugged her arms tightly around herself.

"Yesterday's Memories."

Oh, God, she despaired as her eyes stung with tears, if only her own memory would come back.

Post-traumatic amnesia. That's what the doctor had called it. But in simple terms, she had lost her memory.

She had lost twenty-four hours out of her life.

And until the memory of those hours returned, she'd never be able to answer the question that had taunted her and shamed her, haunted and bedevilled her, for every waking moment since the day she'd discovered she was pregnant.

Who was the father of her child?

CHAPTER SIX

NEXT morning, Megan woke up with a raspy throat and the sniffles.

"You can't go 'round to Jodi's this afternoon," Kendra said. "Not if you're coming down with a cold. You'd only risk spreading it."

But when she phoned to cancel Megan's visit, Brodie told her Jodi had a bit of a cold, too.

"Bring Megan 'round," he said. "I'll keep them inside. They'll be OK...and happier to have each other for company."

Kendra took one look at Megan's pleading face, and gave in.

"All right," she murmured. "We'll be there at two."

When they arrived at the Calder Street house, Brodie came out to meet them. He was wearing an unbuttoned shirt over cut-off jeans. His feet were bare and his hair was wet.

When he leaned into the car, through Kendra's open window, she smelled chlorine. He must have just come out of the pool, she thought.

"Hi, there," he greeted her. And to Megan he said, "Go 'round the back way, poppet. Jodi's in the kitchen."

Megan grabbed the box of tissues her mother thrust at her and took off.

"Thanks," Kendra said to Brodie. "Well, I'll be getting along now..."

"It's not much fun in a motel room on a Saturday night," he said. "Come over and join us for dinner."

She knew she should come up with some excuse, but her mind had become suddenly blank. "We're going to be in the motel for a lot of nights," she finally said. "We'd better get used to it! Besides, I don't want to impose."

"You wouldn't be imposing."

She felt herself drowning in his eyes. For one long helpless moment. And then her brain lurched to attention. What was she *thinking* of? She didn't want to get tangled with this man. Oh, she couldn't deny she was attracted to him; and he certainly *appeared* to be similarly attracted to her. But she could never get seriously involved with him. To have any kind of honest relationship, she'd have to tell him her secret...and she could just imagine the gloating expression in his eyes if she did.

The snooty Westmore brat really got her comeuppance!

That would be his opinion and he wouldn't be backward in expressing it! But she'd never let it happen. She had more than her fair share of pride and she'd *never* put herself in a position where Brodie Spencer—or any other man!—could crow over her misfortunes.

"No, I'll pick Megan up before you eat dinner," she said. "She'll be ready for an early night, I think."

Her voice was as stiff as if she'd starched it!

He raised his eyebrows, but didn't argue.

"Come along around six then. I'll have Megan ready."

He sounded as cool as she had. A total turnaround from the friendly way he'd welcomed her.

It was probably for the best, she decided as she drove away; the more distance she put between them—both physically and emotionally!—the safer she would surely be!

From Brodie's place she drove to Rosemount to interview the four gardeners who had answered her ad.

She conducted the interviews outside, in the trellised gazebo by the water fountain. She ended up hiring the last applicant on the list, a middle-aged local man called Frank Young. He offered excellent references, including a glowing one from Dr. Jamieson, whose gardens he'd tended for years.

Kendra was well pleased with her choice, and stood chatting with the man beside his van before he left.

"I hear you plan on running Rosemount as a B and B." Frank puffed on his pipe and squinted up at the house through the fragrant veil of blue-gray smoke. "It's a big house, all right. How many rooms do you have, Ms. Westmore?"

"Six bedrooms upstairs and one on the main floor. Then there are two smaller ones in the servants' quarters."

"Well, I wish you luck in your venture." He opened his van door. "Tis a pity, all the same, that it's strangers you'll be entertaining here. It's a grand old place, no doubt about it...but something of a mausoleum, if you don't mind my saying so." He climbed into the van, shut the door, and added through the open window, "It needs bringing to life, and there's nothing like a bunch of kids around a place to do that!" His eyes twinkled. "Me and the wife, we've got seven, and I can tell you, there's nothing like a bunch of kids to make a house into a home.

Well—'' he fired the engine ''—much appreciate you hiring me, Ms. Westmore. I'll look forward to working here, it'll be a real treat.''

Kendra stood in the drive till the van had disappeared, before wandering into the house, feeling vaguely depressed.

But why should that be? She had achieved what she'd hoped to this afternoon: she'd hired a gardener who was exactly the kind of person she'd been looking for.

It took her a few minutes to realize that her depression was on account of Frank Young's remark that it was a pity she'd be entertaining strangers here...and that it took a bunch of kids to turn a house into a home.

What he'd said had touched a tender place deep inside her, one she rarely visited. Oh, she would create a private and cozy corner of Rosemount for herself and Megan—but wouldn't it be wonderful to run the lovely white mansion as a *family* home instead of a B and B; catering to husband and children rather than guests who would pass through like ships in the night!

She walked upstairs and wandered restlessly from room to room. All the bedrooms had a view of the lake; all were elegantly furnished—as they always had been—and would require little or no refurbishing to prepare them for paying guests.

She stood in the doorway of the master bedroom, and then slumped against the doorjamb, closing her eyes.

She listened.

And the silence was deafening.

She tried to imagine how it would be to hear children's voices shouting, laughing, teasing, fighting.

She tried to image how it would be to hear a man's voice, calling, "Kendra? Are you there? I'm home, honey!"

She felt her heart ache, her eyes smart.

Swallowing a lump in her throat, she blinked back the threatening tears and pushed herself abruptly from the doorjamb.

Dreams. That's all they were.

Just dreams.

And she'd stopped believing in dreams, a long time ago.

Hayley brought Megan to the front door when Kendra went to pick her up.

"You've missed Brodie," the teenager said as she walked with Kendra and Megan to the Honda. "He went out a little while ago."

Well, he'd timed that nicely, Kendra thought. In order to avoid her, of course. And who could blame him, after the snarky way she'd talked to him? But that's what she wanted, wasn't it, to avoid being in his company?

Then why was she feeling...disappointed?

"Please thank him for having Megan." She bundled Megan into the car and closed the door. "I heard you weren't too well yourself, last night. You're OK now?"

"Fine thanks. I felt badly about letting Jodi down, though—but when I got up this morning she told me Brodie had filled in. That was so sweet of him. He missed most of the hockey game on TV and he'd been looking forward to it all week."

This new information about Brodie tugged a couple

of Kendra's heartstrings. The man was almost too good to be true.

"He's the best," Hayley said, as if she could read Kendra's mind. "Absolutely the A-1 best." Her cheeks became rose-pink. "He'd make a wonderful husband...but it would have to be the right woman—"

She stopped abruptly and looked beyond Kendra as the sound of an approaching vehicle throbbed in the evening air. Without looking around, Kendra knew it was Brodie's truck.

"Well, I'm going in now." Hayley's cheeks had deepened to the same crimson as her sweatshirt. "It's time Jodi was in bed." She darted off with a quick, "'Bye!"

Kendra stared dazedly after the teenager. Hayley's message couldn't have been plainer: Brodie's up for grabs and as far as I'm concerned, you're welcome to go after him.

Unbelievable!

Brodie pulled his truck up alongside her car on the wide driveway. He jumped down and said, "I'm glad I caught you." He opened the white paper bag in his hands and took out a bottle of medicine.

"I got one each for the kids. Joanne at the drugstore said it would soothe the sore throats."

The evening sun played peek-a-boo in his hair, and bronzed his face. Kendra had never denied to herself that the man was ruggedly attractive, but now when she looked at him she saw more. She saw past the exterior perfection to what lay below the surface.

And when she did, she wanted to weep.

The Brodie Spencer who used to raise hell in Lakeview was lost forever. Life had taken him by the scruff of the neck—black leather jacket and all—and shaken the boy out of him.

He was all man now.

But she ached for the boy that was. He'd been a free spirit, and free spirits were to be admired and envied because they were a very special breed.

"What's up?" he asked. "You're looking at me as if I'm a stranger to you! Not," he added with a return to his familiar mocking tone, "that it would be the first time!"

He was surely referring, of course, to the many times she'd treated him with disdain! She ignored his gibe.

"That was sweet of you to think of Megan, too. Thanks."

"Sweet?" He rolled his eyes and his lips twitched. "Good grief!" He looked around with an air of fake furtiveness. "Don't let anybody hear you say that. My reputation would go down the drain! Despite what you may have read to the contrary, today's woman isn't looking for sweet—she's looking for macho!"

"Do you *have* a woman in your life, Brodie?" Kendra could hardly believe the question had popped from her own mouth. She would have bitten it back but it was too late.

"Not at the moment. Why do you ask?"

His gaze seemed to bore right into her mind and sift through all the thoughts stumbling around in confusion.

"Well, you're..." She reached for an answer, but the only one she could come up with was the point Hayley had reportedly made to her friend Zoe. "Men have needs." The answer came out defiantly.

When she saw the twinkle in his eyes, she wished

the driveway would open up so she could drop to the Antipodes and never come back. She glanced around with a sense of desperation...and saw that Megan's face was pressed to the car window, nose flattened, eyes aglitter with curiosity.

"I do have needs." Brodie's fingers tightened on her arm. "But...I had no idea you were...interested in them."

"I'm not!" She tilted her face up. "I am *not* interested in your needs!"

His smile was wicked. "You used to be..."

"I did not!"

"Then who was the girl that used to watch from behind the Rosemount curtains when I worked half-naked in the Westmore gardens those long-ago summers?"

"You're talking nonsense!" But her skin had become warm from the tips of her breasts right up to her hairline. "I had more to do than watch you—"

"And you used to fantasize about me! You used to wonder how it would feel to touch my bare back, slide your palms over the smooth tanned skin, the hard muscles—"

Kendra jerked herself free. "You have a wonderful imagination, Brodie Spencer!" Her face now felt like flame. "But I'll thank you to keep it to yourself...especially when there are children around!"

"You know damned well Megan can't hear me through those windows!" Still grasping her shoulder, he walked her around to the driver's side. He grabbed the handle of her door, but didn't open it. Pulling her close, he hissed in her ear, "Yes, I have needs, damn you! And one of these days I'll remind you of how passionate those needs are!"

He opened the car door and she slid—rather fell!—into her seat.

As she fumbled breathlessly for the ignition key, he leaned over her and said to Megan in a voice that was rich with warmth and light as the evening breeze, "Honey, I hope you feel better soon. Take care now!"

Then he slammed the door without addressing Kendra again, and strode away without once looking back.

How on earth had he guessed she used to watch him?

Kendra felt her shirt stick to her back as perspiration popped out all over her skin. It had been a stab in the dark, must have been...but it had hit the mark. Damn the man! He was too perspicacious for his own good...

Certainly too perspicacious for hers.

As she drove along the street toward the motel, she was scarcely aware of Megan talking to her.

Not till she heard her daughter say, "And Jodi's Dad's going away tomorrow night," did her ears perk up.

"Away? Where's he going?"

"Toronto. To a big trade show. It's where he sees all sorts of new stuff and puts in orders for his company."

"Will he be gone long?"

"He'll be back Friday night. Jodi said *she's* going to be really busy next week helping in the house 'cos Hayley has to do cookery demonstrations at school every morning for a course she's taking *plus* Hayley's got oodles of homework now she's in grade twelve and she wants to stay on the Honor Roll so she can get into one of the best universities."

"You like Hayley, don't you!"

"Yup, she's nice to me. Jodi's lucky having a big sister. And a brother. And a dog, of course."

"I could never have a dog when I was little. My grandfather was allergic to them." Kendra pulled into the motel car park. "Maybe," she said, "once we get settled back in the house, we could think about getting a dog."

"Oh, I like Fetch. Fact, I already love him." Megan unclicked her seat belt. She paused for a series of sneezes. "You don't have to bother getting a dog for me. I'll be over at Jodi's a lot. She said he can be my dog, too."

As they walked into the motel foyer, uneasiness settled over Kendra like a cloud. Megan was really getting herself entrenched in the Spencer household. It was incredible; she'd only known Jodi for six days, and already they were as close as if they'd been best buddies for years.

Kendra sighed. How on earth would she manage to avoid Brodie when their daughters were fast becoming inseparable!

Sunday it rained.

And Megan's cold had become worse.

Monday morning, it was worse still. Kendra phoned the school office to say her daughter wouldn't be in that day.

She'd no sooner put the phone down than it rang. It was Hayley. And she sounded very distraught.

"Hayley? What's wrong?"

"This is an awful imposition but...I want to ask if you could do me a huge favor."

"Well...sure, if I can..."

"It's Jodi, she's still got this awful cold and headache and sore throat...and well, she can't possibly go to school, and I just have to be there today because I've got this presentation to do." Hayley took in a deep breath and then went on with more than a hint of desperation in her tone, "Our regular sitter's out of town—could you *possibly* come over here and baby-sit?"

Twenty minutes later, Kendra was tucking a drowsy Megan into the empty twin bed in Jodi's room. Jodi herself was in a deep sleep.

After a lingering glance at Megan, Kendra followed Hayley from the room.

"I've got to run," Hayley said apologetically as they descended the stairs. "Will you manage? You know where the kitchen is, and the sitting room and—"

"I'll find my way around." Kendra shooshed Hayley toward the entranceway. "Where's Jack?"

"He left at eight." Hayley snatched a yellow slicker from the closet. "He had band practice. We'll both be home around four-thirty. You can contact me at school if need be—phone the office, they'll call me on the P.A. system."

A minute later, Kendra was alone, except for two sick children, in Brodie Spencer's house.

Brodie showered and changed after his first day at the trade show, and then watched the evening news on TV.

When it was over, he clicked off the set and wandered to the window. Wearily, he stared down at the street miles below—miniature figures scurrying along sidewalks, toy vehicles jammed bumper-to-bumper on all of the six lanes.

A city of strangers.

When had he stopped enjoying these out-of-town trips? Because he had, at one time, enjoyed them! God, how he'd enjoyed them! In the beginning. When he was still railing against the malevolent Fates that had not only deprived him of half his family, but had decreed that he settle down.

He pressed his warm palms on the cold pane of glass and his gaze lost its focus as memories drifted into his mind.

Memories of Laurie.

She'd been a salesperson for a Toronto firm, that first year he'd attended the trade show. She'd been seven years older than he was, but sexual attraction had sparked between them on sight. They'd gone to bed within hours of that first meeting, and had enjoyed a sporadic affair over the next few years, rendezvousing in either Vancouver or Toronto, whenever Laurie's hectic schedule permitted.

Then fifteen months ago it had all stopped. Laurie had been promoted to a plum position in Halifax—a position that involved no traveling. They had decided to call it a day.

He'd missed her, vaguely. But their relationship had been based solely on sex, so he didn't miss her as a person.

She'd filled a need.

That was all.

And it had worked both ways. She was a city girl

and she'd often told him she'd rather eat dead worms than marry a man who lived in a hick town in the middle of nowhere!

Marriage had never been on his mind, either. Laurie Campbell was a career woman first, last and always; a bold voluptuous brunette, sexy as hell...and after a couple of drinks, oftentimes a little coarse. Definitely not the type to take home and introduce to the kids!

The kids.

He refocused his eyes. And his thoughts. Shifted them to home...and to Jodi.

How was she doing? That was some awful cold she'd come down with. No chance she'd have gone to school today. Hayley would've had to call Mrs. Thomas.

He looked at the radio-alarm on his bedside table: 7:05. Five after four, Pacific time. He'd call home, and then he'd go down to the bar for a cold beer.

Sitting on the edge of the mattress, he put the call through. A moment later, he heard the dial tone.

Mrs. T. would be in the sitting room, ensconced in his big leather chair, a section of the *Vancouver Sun* folded on her lap and open at the *New York Times*'s crossword.

A wry smile inched over his face. How he wished he was relaxing in his own chair right now!

The phone was lifted at the other end. And a very familiar voice—but certainly not the lilting Welsh voice of their regular baby-sitter—said, "Spencer residence."

Brodie jerked the phone away from his ear and stared at it in outrage...as if it had bitten him.

Kendra Westmore!

What the *hell* was that woman doing in his house?

CHAPTER SEVEN

KENDRA frowned.

"Hello?" she said. "Hellooo?"

Nothing from the other end of the phone line.

She was just about to return the receiver to the cradle when she heard a man's voice—a very familiar voice—say, "Kendra? What the hell's going on!"

She sagged against the kitchen wall.

She'd thought, when the phone rang, that it might be Hayley. She hadn't anticipated that it might be Brodie...

And she couldn't have known that just the sound of his voice would make her knees wobble.

"Brodie?" She reached with one hand for a kitchen chair, and pulling it over, slumped onto it.

"What's up?" he demanded. "Is something wrong?"

"Your Mrs. Thomas couldn't baby-sit." She stared at the tray of hot cinnamon buns she'd just taken out of the oven. "Hayley called me this morning, asked if I could fill in."

She heard nothing for six heartbeats.

Then, "You're baby-sitting? At my house?"

It was there, that slyly taunting note that so often threaded his words when he talked to her. The words themselves not offensive; but what was between the lines was: *So the snooty Westmore brat's baby-sitting the Spencer kids! Isn't that a turn-up for the books!*

She bit back the haughty retort that flew to her lips. "I had to bring Megan. She's still sick, too."

"Then I really owe you." The taunting note was gone. "Look, I'm sorry about all this. It's my fault. I should have checked with Mrs. T. last night before I left. Should have made sure she was available just in case—"

"No use crying over spilled milk, Brodie." Kendra spoke briskly. "I'm glad you called though. I'm going to ask Dr. Jamieson to have a look at Megan. I wondered…is he your family doctor?"

"Yeah, he's our doctor. And I'd appreciate if you'd ask him to give Jodi a once-over, too. And don't hesitate to get in touch with me if you think it's necessary. Are you in the sitting room?"

"No, the kitchen."

'My hotel number's there, on the corkboard."

"I see it."

"OK. That's it then? Hayley and Jack fine?"

"I haven't seen Jack, he'd left for school before I got here. But yes, I think everything else is fine."

"Tell Hayley I'll call her tomorrow morning, around seven your time."

"Brodie, I've been thinking…"

"Yeah?"

"Mrs. T.'s out of town for a while. If the doctor says Jodi ought not to go to school tomorrow, it would be easier all 'round if I stay the night here. Megan's got a fever, I don't want to be hauling her out of bed and taking her back and forth from the motel. And it would be easier for Hayley, knowing I'm here."

"You wouldn't mind?"

"No. As I say…it would be easier."

"Ms. Westmore, I'm in your debt and I like to pay my debts. When I get back, I'll treat you to a big night out on the town! Cocktails, dinner, dancing, at the place of your choice in beautiful downtown Lakeview!"

"Gee, Brodie, you sure know how to treat a girl! You mean I get to choose between the Red Barn Lounge and McCoogan's Hoedown Bar?"

"Don't be sarcastic, Westmore, it doesn't suit you. And I'll have you know there've been a lot of changes in our little town since you took off for greener pastures. You go out with me, honey, I promise you won't be disappointed."

After Kendra had put the phone down, the teasing huskiness of his voice lingered in her ears, and she felt excitement, unwanted excitement, sizzling in her veins.

A night on the town with Brodie Spencer.

That would surely set tongues wagging! She could almost hear them now. The Westmore girl on a date with that wild Spencer boy!

Except that she was no longer a girl, and Brodie was no longer a boy. Nor was he wild.

What he was was irresistibly attractive, infuriatingly superior—and in every way that mattered, incredibly decent.

She admired him tremendously...

And, she admitted with a flush, she liked him, too.

A lot.

The way he was now.

Yet something, somewhere deep inside of her, ached to see him just once more on the back of his Harley-Davidson motorbike; roaring through town in his black leather jacket; answering to nobody.

Just one more time.

"So," Dr. Jamieson said, when he came round that evening, "my receptionist tells me you're baby-sitting while Brodie's out of town." He looked at Kendra over top of his half-glasses as she hung his rain-spattered coat in the hall closet. "Edward Westmore would turn in his grave if he knew his granddaughter was hobnobbing with the Spencer family!"

"Let him turn!" Kendra said lightly, and ushered him toward the stairs.

She hadn't seen the doctor since the day of her grandfather's funeral, and they hadn't had a chance to talk privately on that occasion...for which she had been thankful. The man knew altogether too much about her—more than anyone in the world, now that her grandfather was gone.

Being in his company made her...uneasy.

She hovered as he examined his patients, and then took the prescriptions he scribbled out for them.

But when she walked to the door, expecting him to follow, he paused at the foot of Jodi's bed and said to the girls, "You're a lucky pair, having company like this when you're sick. You in the same class at school?"

"Yes, doctor," croaked Jodi. "And we're both the same age. Well, Megan's a bit older than I am. My birthday's not till December but Megan's going to be eight in October."

Kendra thought her heart was going to stop. She grasped the edge of the door as she felt her legs wobble.

Had the doctor realized the implications of what Jodi had said?

She prayed silently, intensely, that he had not.

He was a good age now; must be in his mid-sixties. Surely his memory wouldn't be as sharp as it had once been.

Eyes fixed desperately on him, she tried to guess if what Jodi had said had jarred him.

But he showed no sign of having noticed anything untoward. She breathed out a sigh of relief, and forcing a smile, escorted him downstairs.

She gave him his coat and he put it on without a word.

She couldn't wait for him to be gone, so she could let her guard down.

Opening the front door, she said, "Thank you for coming, Doctor. I'll make sure the girls take it easy."

"This bug they've got can turn nasty if it's neglected. They should stay home from school for the rest of the week. Call me if either one takes a turn for the worse."

"I will." Go, she ordered him silently. Please go.

He walked out to the stoop, and turned.

"Kendra." He put a hand on her shoulder and his gaze was blunt and probing. "Did you miscarry that baby?"

She knew which baby he was talking about. Numbly she shook her head and felt tears sting her eyes.

"I thought not." His expression was weary. "Honey, I've been a doctor for forty years and in all that time I've never had a patient whose pregnancy lasted twelve months. I'm sure you must have a very good reason for lying about Megan's age, but one day you're going to have to tell her the truth. In the meantime, your secret's safe with me, and should you ever want to talk—well, you know where my office is. The same place it was when you came to see me that Christmas Eve eight years ago."

After he'd gone, Kendra went into the sitting room and crossed to the window. A strong wind had arisen and was lashing the rain against the panes. The panes shuddered.

Just as she herself shuddered.

The past flooded into her mind, and pain twisted her heart as she recalled the visit Dr. Jamieson was referring to. It was on that visit she'd learned something that had shattered her girlhood dreams, and changed her life forever.

She'd come home to Rosemount for Christmas; and had decided it was time to see a doctor. She hadn't menstruated since early September and at first she'd blamed that on her accident, then later put it down to the stress of her first term at university. But for the past few weeks she'd been feeling vaguely unwell, so she made an appointment to see Dr. Jamieson. The only available slot was late on the afternoon of the twenty-fourth.

When she left his office, it was in a state of shock. But on the heels of shock came anxiety and apprehension. She'd have to tell her grandfather. And there was no point in putting it off, he would find out eventually. She'd stumbled from the clinic, hardly aware of anything or anybody on the street.

She'd gone straight home.

When she'd confessed to her grandfather that she was pregnant, he'd said she was a disgrace to the family name...and he'd *demanded* to know who the baby's father was.

She'd wept that she didn't know.

She'd tried to explain; he wouldn't listen.

With rage mottling his handsome face, he'd shouted at her to get out, that she was no longer welcome in his house.

She had taken him at his word.

None of it would have happened if she hadn't gone to Seattle in late September that year, for a weekend with Ashleigh.

The Black Bats, her favorite rock group, were performing at a charity concert in Merivale Park, just outside Seattle. Her nineteen-year-old cousin worked in the city, and had an apartment there; and when she'd phoned to say she had two tickets for the Saturday concert and did Kendra want to join her, Kendra had been thrilled to accept.

Ashleigh wasn't really a cousin, she was from a distant branch of the Westmore family. Kendra's grandfather had severed relations with them after Ashleigh's father and mother were involved in a scandalous divorce. Ashleigh had been thirteen at that time; Kendra eleven. But unknown to Kendra's grandfather, the girls had secretly kept in touch, although they had little in common. Ashleigh eventually left school at sixteen and took a job in a Seattle beauty salon. Kendra graduated from Lakeview High with honors when she was seventeen, and at the time of Ashleigh's invitation she was just over a month into her freshman year at U.B.C., and living in residence at the university.

The concert was to start on the Saturday at noon.

Kendra had bused down to Seattle from Vancouver the previous evening, and she and Ashleigh set out early on Saturday for Merivale Park in Ashleigh's red Probe. The day was already brilliantly sunny and very hot, and the enormous grassy field was jammed with people when they got there.

A parking attendant directed Ashleigh to a parking spot under a gigantic willow tree close by a gate marked Exit 4. As she and Ashleigh walked from the Probe, Ashleigh said, "If by chance we should get separated, and can't find each other again, we'll meet here immediately after the concert's over. We'll beat the rush that way, since we're right close to an exit. Take a good look at the layout, Kenny—remember it good so's you can find your own way back if you have to."

Kendra looked around. She took note of the huge willow and its situation in relation to the enormous stage in the far corner of the field. And she remembered saying to herself, "It's by Exit 4. Under the big willow. Kitty-corner to the stage."

She did "remember it good."

It was also the last thing she was later to remember of that day.

The following morning she'd awakened in a Seattle hospital with an injured hip and a concussion.

Ashleigh was by her bedside, her face drawn and gray.

"Kenny!" Ashleigh grabbed Kendra's hand when she saw her eyes open. "Thank God you're awake. How do you feel?"

"Ashleigh?" Kendra felt dazed, her voice sounded road-gravel raspy. "What's...what's going on?"

"You're in hospital, Kenny. We were in an accident on the way back to my place after the concert—

not my fault,'' she hastened to add. ''An old guy had a heart attack and ran right through a stop sign. You've been out cold ever since. Kenny—'' Ashleigh's eyes were evasive ''—I know it was a dirty trick, taking off with Gavin and leaving you on your own. I just feel awful now. But it all worked out, didn't it, 'cos you did say you'd met somebody and had a wonderful time—''

Kendra hadn't the first clue what her cousin was talking about! ''Ashleigh.'' She clutched her cousin's hand. ''I don't remember *anything* about what you're saying! I don't remember the concert, or anybody called Gavin—and I don't remember any crash. You left me alone—and I met somebody?'' Tears welled up in her eyes. ''I don't remember!''

''Don't worry,'' Ashleigh soothed. ''It'll all come back.''

A sudden panicky thought pierced Kendra's foggy brain. ''Grandfather...he doesn't know, does he? You haven't called him?''

''No, no!'' Ashleigh rolled her eyes. ''Can you imagine what he'd say if he knew you were down here? At a rock concert? And with me?'' Her laugh was cynical. ''Don't worry, Kenny. I told the admitting clerk I was your next of kin. This will be our secret, now and forever.''

Kendra ran the tip of her tongue over her parched lips. ''Thanks, Ash.'' She smiled weakly. ''I 'preciate that.'' Among all the questions blundering around in the dark mists of her mind, one demanded to be answered. ''But...who was I with...at the concert...after you left?''

''I don't know. We met up at the car when the concert was over...like we'd arranged...and I guess I was so busy talking about Gavin—I'd always had a thing for him but kept clear 'cos he was married, anyway his wife's left him and—'' She grimaced. ''I was being selfish like always, talking about myself, and then when I finally apologized for leaving you in the lurch, you said it was OK, you'd met somebody—''

''*Who?*''

Ashleigh's expression was apologetic. ''Kenny, I don't know. All I do know is that you were happy, happiest I've ever seen you. You were just glowing with it...and you were just about to tell me *everything,* when wham!'' She twisted her index finger nervously around a strand of her kinky red hair. ''That car rammed into us from out of the blue. I was shaken up a bit, that's all...but you...well, you've had this concussion. And your hip got hurt. My insurance will cover everything, Kenny...and you should get a nice lump sum for pain and s—''

A door slammed and the sound was so sharp it jumped Kendra from the past—from the Seattle hospital room—to where she was now, in the sitting room of Brodie Spencer's house. From almost nine years ago to the present day. In the blink of an eye.

She realized she was rubbing her fingertips over her right hip, as if it still pained her, whereas other than the faint scars, there was nothing at all to remind her that her hip had ever been injured.

She heard a scuffle out in the foyer. That must be Jack—he'd gone out after dinner to take Fetch for a run in the rain.

With a sigh she moved across the room. And pasting on a smile, she went out to the hall.

Fetch was meandering off in the direction of the kitchen. Jack was unzipping his jacket.

"Hi," she greeted him.

"Oh, hi, Ms. Westmore. You're still here?"

She explained about the girls having to stay home from school for the rest of the week and told him she was going to baby-sit for as long as she was needed.

"Cool!" he said.

"Dr. Jamieson left a couple of prescriptions. Would you mind biking to the drugstore and getting them filled?"

"Sure, no problem."

Hayley was upstairs doing her homework, and when Kendra went to fill her in on what was happening, she was gratified when the teenager gave her an impulsive hug as she thanked her.

"We don't have a guest room," Hayley said. "I'll make up the sofa bed in the den. You won't hear the girls from there so I'll listen for them. And I'm afraid Fetch sleeps in the den. I hope he doesn't bother you too much with his snuffling. There's no point in shoving him into the hall and closing him out—he'll just whine till you let him back in!"

"Don't worry," Kendra said. "Fetch won't bother me."

When Jack came back, she gave the girls their medicine and settled them down for the night. She herself went to bed at eleven and was asleep within minutes. She didn't hear a thing till Hayley's wake-up call in the morning—neither Fetch's "snufflings" nor the gale, which Hayley told her over breakfast had continued to howl through the night.

The wild weather continued for the next couple of days, but Thursday dawned fine and fair. Though there was a distinct nip of autumn in the air, by midday the sun had burned it away and the town shimmered under a heat haze.

Megan and Jodi were both on the mend, and Kendra let them come downstairs that evening to watch TV. When she was tucking them in for the night later, Megan said, hopefully, "Tomorrow can we go to school?"

"No, honey, Dr. Jamieson said Monday. You know that."

Jodi sighed. "Well, at least Dad'll be home tomorrow night. I sure miss him."

"What time do you expect him home?" Kendra asked.

"Evening. Hayley said around seven."

Good, thought Kendra. She'd stay here till Hayley got home from school, then she and Megan would go back to the motel.

That way she'd be long gone before Brodie got home.

Brodie slid his key into the front door lock and eased it around gently.

He pushed open the door and in the moonlight, slipped into the foyer and closed the door behind him.

He set his travel bag on the floor beside the closet, took off his shoes, and flicked on the hall light.

Lord, was he ever tired! His plane had been an hour late arriving in Vancouver, and the drive up the Coquihalla had been even more tedious than usual—

He blinked as he looked around the foyer.

Had he walked into the wrong house?

He scratched his head as his astonished gaze skimmed over the floor, searching for all the junk that had normally collected there by the time Thursday night rolled around!

The Widow Westmore had been busy! Now she would be sound asleep in the den...and she wouldn't be expecting him till tomorrow. She'd get quite a shock when he turned up at the breakfast table!

Slinging his jacket over the newel post at the foot of the stairs, he clicked off the hall light and walked along the shadowy corridor toward the kitchen.

As he passed the den, he heard a scratching sound, and a faint whimper.

Dammit, Fetch must have heard the truck.

Brodie opened the door carefully. The room was in total darkness. He felt Fetch's rough tongue on his hand, felt the solid body brush his leg as the dog padded by him.

Brodie followed him to the kitchen. In the moonlight slanting in through the uncurtained window, he crossed the room and let the dog out the door to the backyard.

He shut the door again...and tensed as he heard a rustling sound from the corridor.

The kitchen light came on unexpectedly, dazzling him as he swiveled around.

Kendra was standing in the doorway.

"Oh!" Her voice was breathless, and husky with sleep. "It's you!"

She looked like a wayward angel. Her blond hair was pillow-tousled, her brown eyes lustrous and wide, her full breasts and flaring hips licked intimately by her white silk robe. Lust dug his jet lag in the ribs, shunting it aside.

"I'm sorry." He cleared his throat. Twice. "I disturbed you? Was it the truck...or when I let Fetch out?"

"I didn't hear the truck. I did hear the den door open. I thought it might be Megan or Jodi, I wanted to check nothing was wrong."

"How've they been?"

"Same as when Hayley spoke to you this morning. They'll be right as rain by Monday, I'm sure."

"Good."

"We weren't expecting you back till tomorrow evening."

"I managed to finish up early so I caught the first available flight home. Hotel rooms...I hate 'em."

"How was your trip?"

What would she think if she knew he'd cut it short simply because he couldn't get her out of his mind? But even his dreams hadn't prepared him for this. "Everything went just fine." He cleared his throat. Again. He tugged down his tie, opened the top couple of buttons of his shirt.

"Do you want...a beer or something?"

Or something, he thought. He wanted to open his arms and have her walk into them. Then he wanted to slide his hands up and down her back, run it through that gloriously disheveled hair, tip her face up to his and plunder that luscious cherry-pink mouth till—

"A beer," he said, "sounds great. But only if you'll stay and have one with me."

Her nose wrinkled, so slightly as to be almost unnoticeable, and then her lips curved in a rueful smile.

"Actually," she murmured, "I wouldn't mind a cold drink. I've been tossing and turning all night. I guess it's the heat."

"It's a hot one, all right." And you can say that again!

She took out two cans of beer and handed one to him. He popped it open.

"Do you need a glass?" she asked as she took one down from the cupboard for herself.

What I need, he thought, is you.

"Nah, this'll do." He waited till she'd poured her beer, then he lifted his can. "Cheers."

"Cheers." She gulped down a mouthful of her drink and the beer frothed her upper lip.

He drank from the can, his gaze never leaving her.

"It's good!" She looked astonished. "I've never drunk beer before...but it's...thirst-quenching, isn't it!"

At her words, a feeling like lead settled deep in the pit of his stomach. "Never?" He kept his voice steady.

She gave a half laugh. "Never. I'm not really a drinker...but when I do have something alcoholic, it's usually wine."

"Well, well." He leaned back against the counter and smiled lazily. "You're quite something, Ms. Westmore. You really are. You'll stand here, in my own kitchen, and tell me to my face that this is the first beer you've ever tasted? In your life?"

Her cheeks flushed. "Are you calling me a *liar?*"

"Are you saying, Ms. Westmore, that you've never even tasted it on some man's lips?"

"That's what I'm saying, Mr. Spencer!"

He put his can down and closed the distance between them in two long strides. Before she could protest, he took her glass from her and set it on the table.

Then he did what he'd been aching to do from the moment she'd switched on the kitchen light.

He hauled her hard against his chest.

And kissed her.

CHAPTER EIGHT

THE TEXTURE of her lips was exquisite. It tantalized him, drove him wild…as did the intoxicating scent of her hair and skin, and the voluptuous upthrust of her breasts.

Dammit, he shouldn't be doing this…but he wanted to get through to her. He wanted to—yes, he admitted it—he wanted to break her, crush her innate stubborn arrogance. She'd denied him…again! And as she did, he'd felt anger explode him from his sensual enjoyment of her company to this raging desire to punish. To kiss till she was his…and then to walk away, unscathed.

And she *was* enjoying the kiss. No doubt about that. Oh, at first her body had stiffened, but as he tightened his embrace and moved his mouth seductively over hers, she began to yield. And in a matter of seconds, with a tiny sound in her throat, she'd twined her arms around his neck and arched up to him.

Yes!

Relentlessly, triumphantly, he deepened the kiss, determined to have her at his feet. Determined to master her. Determined to make her beg.

He wove his fingers through her hair, whispered urgent nothings in her ear, framed her face in his hands…felt her cheeks petal-soft against his palms…

She'd parted her full moist lips and he slid his tongue into her mouth. She gasped, and then with a whimper, dug her nails into the flesh at his nape…like a cat with claws. A blond cat, sleek, purring, hot…

Need rushed through him like a hurricane, and he felt himself go rock-hard.

With a jarring shock, he realized he was losing control. Fast. If he didn't stop this…and stop it now…he'd take it all the way. Because he couldn't help himself. And *that* was not in his plan.

What a sucker he was for her! He hated feeling like this—that he no longer had the power.

Reeling from the knowledge of his vulnerability, he grasped her upper arms and held her away from him.

"I'm sorry," he said, trying to keep his voice steady. "That was a mistake." He somehow managed to shape his mouth into a wry grin. "I don't usually make sexual advances to the baby-sitter. Of course, Mrs. T.'s a sixty-something grandmother, so the temptation's never been there before!"

He felt a wave of remorse when he saw the bruised expression in her eyes. Her lips looked bruised, too; how tender that flesh was, to be so wounded after just a few kisses. And her breasts were tender—they quivered under the silk robe, the beaded nipples pouting for the caresses they'd been promised then denied.

He ached to run his palms over them, give them ease. At the thought, the tightening in his groin increased till it almost made him flinch. He could only hope that she didn't lower her gaze, see how she had affected him. She wasn't the only one, he thought, whose flesh was tender—

From outside came two sharp yelps.

Fetch wanted to come in. Brodie latched onto the heaven-sent opportunity to turn his back on this beguiling temptress and get himself cooled down.

"Excuse me," he said.

And took his time opening the door.

The Labrador bounded past him and when Brodie turned back into the room, he saw Kendra had gone. He cocked his head and listened...and heard her walking quickly to the den.

Fetch ignored him and shot after her.

A moment later Brodie heard the den door click shut.

Dammit, he thought as he raked a shaking hand through his hair, that was a close call. He'd have to rethink his plan to get the Widow Westmore into his bed and then walk.

She'd burned him once.

If he wasn't careful, she would burn him again!

Kendra was in the kitchen next morning, making pancakes, when she heard footsteps in the corridor. Brodie's.

She dropped the spoon in her hand, and jumped as it fell to the floor with a clatter. Flustered, she picked it up and slotted it in the dishwasher rack. As she closed the door, Brodie came into the room.

Her heart thudded as she took in his lean powerful figure, his hair damp from his shower. He was wearing a white tank top and black shorts, and a pair of leather thongs. His jaw was smoothly shaven; his eyes—more blue than green today—cool as they skimmed over her, taking in her perky ponytail, her yellow shirt and snug jeans, with an appearance of total uninterest.

"Morning." His tone was casual. "Sleep well?"

Just as if the kiss had never happened! But she certainly wasn't about to give him the satisfaction of knowing the memory of it had kept her awake half the night, one moment in a ferment of longing, the next in a frenzy of resentment at his rejection of her.

"Never better!" Her tone was equally casual.

"Good." His muscles rippled as he took down a mug from the shelf and crossed to the coffeemaker.

The kitchen was about fifteen feet square, but now that he was in it, it seemed to have shrunk to the size of a telephone kiosk. And even though the window was wide open, she felt deprived of air. *He* might find it easy to play this "let's pretend it never happened" game. She did not.

"What do you like for breakfast?" she asked. "Bacon and eggs? Pancakes? Toast? Sausages and tomato?"

"Yeah," he said. "That would be great."

Despite herself, a smile twitched her lips. He hadn't realized she'd been giving him a choice.

"Can I pour you a coffee?" he asked.

"Thanks." She scooped up the pancakes from the frypan, and slid them onto a plate. "I take cream." She cracked two eggs into the pan, and as they sizzled, she added a sliced tomato. From the oven she removed the platter of crisply grilled sausages she'd put there to keep warm.

She straightened and found Brodie beside her, holding out a mug of coffee. He smelled of shampoo and soap. Very clean, very...civilized. So why were her nerves screaming out an alarm, as if he were a caveman who would at any moment grab her by the hair and pull her to his dark lair?

Avoiding his eyes, she took the mug and felt a quiver of relief as he moved away from her and sat at the table.

The children hadn't come down yet; the place settings were still tidy. In the center of the table sat the bowl of pansies she'd cut from one of the flower beds when she'd let Fetch out. And in a basket, fragrant and still steaming from the oven, lay a mound of whole-wheat muffins.

"A man," Brodie drawled as he tilted back his chair, "could get used to this."

Had he ever looked sexier? She took a sip of her coffee, told her pulse to slow down. "What?"

"Coming down to a peaceful kitchen—" his gaze was lazy "— with fresh flowers on the table and a pretty woman serving breakfast."

"Hire yourself a housekeeper, Brodie!" she said pertly.

"I've been thinking about that lately."

"Why haven't you done it before? I mean…you all have busy lives, and you've said yourself that things get pretty messy around here by Friday…so why not have someone in?"

He tilted his chair forward and the front legs clicked on the floor. He cupped his hands around his mug and looked at her. "In the beginning," he said, "when I moved in here, it was important that things stay the same, at least as much the same as possible, for the kids' sake. I wanted to hire a housekeeper, but Hayley didn't want a woman in the house." He lifted his shoulders in a shrug. "In her mother's kitchen."

"Taking her mother's place," Kendra said slowly. "I can understand that. She would…want to take that place herself."

"Yeah, that was it, I think. Heck, the kid wasn't yet twelve, but her mind was set on it. And she was right. It was a good decision to make. It brought us all even closer, because there was no...outsider...to come between."

"But now?"

"You were almost a stranger to the kids. How did they take it, your being here all week? Running the household?"

He hadn't answered her question; but she knew why he'd asked the one he did. "They've liked it, I think. It's made things go...smoothly."

"Yeah." He raked back his hair and somehow she thought there was a weariness in the gesture. "I've been planning to broach the subject of hiring somebody. Soon."

Kendra wondered if she should mention anything about Hayley going to college next year. She decided against it. It was none of her business. But she wished she could erase the frown from Brodie's brow. Wished she had the right to lean over, plant a kiss on his hair, twine her arms around his neck—

Oh, sure...and look what had happened last night when she'd twined her arms around his neck!

She jerked herself round and returned her attention to the pan. "Sunny-side up?" she asked.

"Yeah, thanks."

She arranged his food attractively on his plate, and set the plate on the table in front of him.

"Hey, this looks great!" His brows had shot up. "Where'd you learn to cook?"

"I took some chef courses in Vancouver."

"After your husband died?"

Her cheeks flushed. "Yes, I took the courses after I was...on my own." Then she moved swiftly to redirect the course of the conversation. "Molly Flynn did all the cooking when I lived at Rosemount, and she wasn't about to share her kitchen with anybody. Not that my grandfather would have let her, even if she had. Anyway...when I left home at seventeen, I didn't know how to boil an egg!"

"You didn't take Home Ec at school?"

"Couldn't fit it in. I had a heavy academic load."

"You had a job then, I take it, in Vancouver?"

"Mmm. I worked as a sous-chef in a small hotel in the West End."

"You left a lot of friends behind, when you moved back here?"

"Just...work friends. We all got along well on the job, but most of us didn't mix, socially, outside it. I built my leisure time activities around Megan. The area where we lived wasn't very nice...not the kind of place where a little girl could go out and play on her own." She sipped from her mug. "That was the main reason I was glad to be coming back to Lakeview. To get her out of the city."

"The B and B—your cooking skills will come in handy there. And Rosemount—you've got room for at least a dozen guests at one time. And the situation up on the hill is ideal."

Before Kendra could respond, Hayley came flying into the kitchen, jacket on, backpack slung over her shoulder.

"Morning, all!" she said cheerfully. "Saw your truck, Brodie...you're back early!" She gave him a hug, then whisking a warm muffin from the basket, she made for the back door. "Gotta dash, I have to get my presentation ready!"

She'd no sooner gone out than Jack skidded into the room in his stocking soles. "Yo, you're back, Dad. Cool. Hi, Kendra—can I have the same as yesterday? But just four pancakes this morning, I'm not that hungry."

Smiling, Kendra put down her mug and dished up Jack's breakfast. As she set his plate in front of him, she said, "Don't forget your packed lunch. It's in the fridge. Now if you'll both excuse me, I want to go up and check on the girls."

"You and I have a dinner date tonight," Brodie called after her as she crossed the kitchen. "I'll pick you up at the motel at seven."

She paused, her hand on the edge of the door. He still wanted to take her out? After last night? Heavens, he'd more or less called her a liar! Oh, he'd been friendly enough just now, but she'd thought he was just being polite. "I can't...there's Megan—"

"Hayley's offered to baby-sit for our night out. I talked to her about it yesterday morning, when I phoned. So I suggest we keep Megan here for one more night, that way you can lie in tomorrow. From what I've seen around here since I came back, you more than deserve it."

He was taking her out because it was "the right thing" to do. A "thank you" dinner.

"You don't *have* to," she said stiffly.

"Yes," he said, "I do."

And she knew, by his tone, that he would not take no for an answer. Brodie Spencer would be beholden to no one.

"Thank you," she said. "I'll be ready at seven."

Brodie arrived at the motel at one minute to seven. He parked, and had walked halfway to the entrance when the revolving doors swung round and his date emerged.

Kendra smiled, tentatively, and gave him a little wave. He kept walking and as he did, his gaze jerked from one stunning detail to the next...and the next...and the next...

That glorious mane of heavy pale hair, swept back over one ear tonight. A stunning black minidress, scoop-necked and sleeveless. Strappy black sandals with funny clunky heels. Those meter-long legs, sun-browned and elegant. And glints of silver at ear, throat and wrist.

She must have been watching for him from the lobby, he thought.

His next thought was, if angels wore black, then this was an angel.

A sinful angel. An angel who told lies.

Liar, liar, pants on fire...

Yeah, you could say *that* again! But the pants on fire were his own!

He cursed under his breath.

On the drive over, he'd made up his mind how he'd act tonight. He'd be pleasant, friendly...but totally indifferent to her, sexually.

But here he was, just walking to meet her, and already he was aching to take her in his arms and—

Dammit! He scowled darkly. How could he fight this thing? This thing called lust!

"Hi," he said gruffly, halting when they met. She was close enough that he could smell her perfume. It floated around him and he was overtaken by an almost overwhelming urge to sniff the air like a dog, then raise his face to the transparent paper moon in the blue evening sky, and howl!

Good God, he told himself, get a grip. You're not an animal!

No? questioned a taunting voice in his head.

"So." Her voice was as light and tantalizingly sweet as her perfume. "Where are you planning to take me?"

Right here! he almost said. *Right here in the car park.*

He managed to bite back the words.

"It's a new place. Out of town a bit. Overlooking the river."

"Sounds nice."

"It is." He cupped her elbow and led her to the car.

"Oh!" She paused and gave his late-model beige Volvo a once-over. "Where's the truck?"

"This may be Hicksville," he said, opening her door, "but even Brodie Spencer doesn't take his dates out to dinner in a truck."

He'd been stung by the implication that he was still the yahoo he'd been eight years ago, and his grim tone had made that plain. Whatever had happened to *pleasant? Friendly? Indifferent?*

His whole plan for the evening was shattering before him and they hadn't even left the car park!

Right, he said to himself as he drove out onto the street, start over. From now.

"You're looking lovely," he said. Hey, that was good. He'd sounded as casual as if he'd been admiring a slab of cheese in a deli window.

"Oh...thanks..."

From the corner of his eye, he could see she was fidgeting with the small black purse on her lap. Her fine-boned fingers opened the silver catch, closed it, opened it...

Nervously.

Now there was a surprise! The Widow Westmore was nervous around him.

"You look good in black," he said. "Only true blonds do." And where the hell had that come from?

"Thanks...again." She crossed her legs. Uncrossed them. Clicked open her purse. Clicked it shut again. "You're...you're looking—" she cleared her throat "—pretty terrific yourself. I've never...seen you in a suit before."

"This old thing?" Good grief, he sounded like a woman! He wanted to pound his head against the steering wheel. "The kids call it my ice-cream suit. The light color, I guess. We used to have an ice-cream truck come round our way in the summer, he—the driver—wore a jacket this same taupe color..."

"But his jacket would have been cotton/polyester," she said with a hint of amusement in her tone. "Whereas your suit is very nice linen."

"Yeah, but crumples like hell." This conversation was surreal. But somehow he'd lost control of it. "Hayley's forever complaining about having to press it after every time I wear it. I guess that's a job for a wife."

Wife? He barely managed to stifle a groan. Now there was a four-letter word he usually avoided like the plague.

Turn the subject around!

Right.

"Did you," he said as he overtook a lumbering pickup, "press linen suits for your husband?"

He wasn't looking at her but he felt the sharp snap of tension in the air.

After a five-second pause, she said, "No."

"Where did you meet him? Was he at U.B.C., too?"

Silence.

"You must have fallen for him like a ton of bricks," he persisted. "To get married so young. Jodi mentioned that Megan has an October birthday. You must have gotten pregnant around Christmas, your first year away from home."

She was turning her small purse over and over in her lap. He threw her a quick glance; saw that she was staring ahead, her body rigid.

"That's right," she said. "Would you mind...I don't want to talk about it."

He was sorry he'd ever brought the subject up and as he'd heard the quiver in her voice he could have bitten out his tongue. What devil had made him press? He frowned, and slowed down as they approached an intersection. It was just that she was always so...evasive. Was it because her marriage had been unhappy?

"One last question," he said quietly, "and then I'll let it lie. I promise." He braked to a halt at the stop sign, and turned in his seat to look at her. "Were you in love with him? Megan's father?"

She turned to him then and her expression made his blood run cold. Her luminous brown eyes were haunted, like those of a fawn caught in a leghold trap.

"I don't know," she whispered.

Kendra placed her crumpled serviette on the table, and glanced tautly at Brodie as he signed the Visa bill.

From the moment he'd scowled at her in the motel car park she'd sensed that the evening was doomed to failure.

What she hadn't anticipated were his relentless demands to know about her past. And when he'd baldly asked if she'd loved Megan's father he'd caught her *completely* off guard.

She'd blurted out the truth, and then had crawled into a shell of silence from which she'd refused to emerge. Eventually he'd retreated into a surly silence of his own.

She could have kicked herself for opening up even that much to him. Why on earth had she? Oh, she knew the answer to that! She'd turned to snap that it was none of his business...but when she'd seen the honest concern in his eyes, her confession had come tumbling out as if it had a mind of its own!

What *was* it about Brodie Spencer that got to her? Lost in confusion, she stared at him as he handed the Visa check to the waitress...and as he looked up at the woman with a casual smile, she suddenly felt tumblers click into place in her brain, like the sweet sound of a safe being cracked.

She was, she realized to her horror, falling in love with him.

No, not *falling* in love with him...

She was *already* in love with him.

In love with Brodie Spencer.

And as her appalled gaze skimmed his black hair, his lean features, his powerful shoulders—she felt dazzled, starstruck...and she wondered groggily if she hadn't been in love with him forever...

He'd accused her once of spying on him as he worked in the Rosemount gardens. Indeed she *had* spied on him. Summer after long hot summer. And she had yearned for him unbearably...but she had somehow blocked that truth from her mind because he'd been forbidden to her.

Forbidden by dint of the deep wide chasm, the societal gap, that had separated them.

In his world, she'd been "the snooty Westmore brat."

In her world, he'd been "the no-good Spencer kid."

It was ironic that now, when she didn't give a tinker's damn about his or anyone else's so-called "status" in society, Brodie Spencer was still forbidden to her, because she couldn't imagine ever telling him her secret.

And how could she ever hope to have an open and honest relationship with any man with that secret separating them?

The chasm was still there. It was still as deep and as wide. Only it had taken a different form.

"Ready?" Brodie's voice broke in on her thoughts.

She swallowed over the aching lump that had risen in her throat. "Yes," she said, "I'm ready."

As they left the table, she said, "Thanks, I enjoyed—"

"The evening was a disaster." His jaw was grimly set. Planting his hand against the small of her back he propelled her toward the door. "Let's get the hell out of here!"

They drove back to the motel in the same bleak silence that had hovered like a black cloud over their dinner.

He parked at the entrance, got out and escorted her to the revolving doors.

She paused. And looked up at him. "I'll come

round for Megan in the morning. What time would be suitable?''

''Any time after nine.''

His tone was rough, but his eyes had a...lost look. She wondered if he was feeling as mixed up as she was. Her heart took a flying lurch as she heard herself say, ''Would you like to come in and have a night-cap?''

''No.'' His response was terse. ''But thanks anyway.''

Cheeks on fire, she swiveled away from him and pushed her way through the revolving doors. How humiliating! But it was just as well he'd turned down her offer. If she'd spent any more time with him, she might have said—or done!—things she would regret in the morning.

Better to get away from him...and keep away from him!

Her clunky sandals thumped rhythmically on the corridor's carpet as she hurried along to her unit. She would soak in a hot bath, she decided, and watch TV in bed.

She double locked her unit door firmly behind her.

Brodie didn't go straight home.

He drove aimlessly around town for a good half hour, feeling more restless than he'd ever felt in his life. The woman was in his blood—like some damned tropical fever!

And how do you get rid of a fever? You just have to wait till it burns itself out. Well, he'd been waiting too damned long! It was time to do something about it.

His brakes squealed as he did a U-turn.

He stopped only once on his way back to the motel, at the beer and wine store on the corner of Main and Savanna.

Three minutes later he knocked on the door of Unit 5.

Nobody answered.

He frowned. Rapped again, harder this time. And glared belligerently at the peephole.

Still no answer.

Had she gone out? But where the devil would she go?

Lips compressed to a thin line, he was already turning to leave when the door swung open.

She stood there, her cheeks flushed, the tips of her hair wet, her feet bare and pink, her curvy figure wrapped in her white silk robe and bathed in gardenia perfume.

Her eyes were wide. "Did you forget someth—"

He pushed past her rudely, strode down the short foyer and into the kitchenette where he thumped his purchases on the kitchen counter. His heart was going like the hammers.

She'd followed him through. She stood in the doorway, clutching the lapels of her robe to her throat with both hands, apprehension shadowing her brown eyes.

"Yeah," he said, "I forgot to say goodnight."

CHAPTER NINE

BRODIE saw a movement in her throat, as if she'd swallowed.

"What's in that bag?" she asked.

"Wine."

Her eyelids flickered. She paused for a long moment, and then said, "You'll find glasses in the cupboard above the stove. Why don't you pour while I get dressed?"

She didn't wait for an answer; was gone before he could tell her not to bother; she looked fabulous as she was!

The glasses were cheap but spotlessly clean. He found a corkscrew in the cutlery drawer.

He jerked out the cork, and tossed it into the plastic-lined garbage container under the sink. He two-thirds filled the glasses. The wine was pale as her hair, and smelled subtly of nuts. And pears.

He heard a clatter in the bedroom. Had she dropped something? Her hairbrush? Was she still nervous of him? Was she wondering what he'd *really* come back for?

He carried the glasses through to the sitting room and set them on the rectangular coffee table. She'd been getting ready for bed. She'd already unfolded the Hide-A-Bed; it was neatly made up, with crisply laundered sheets, fresh white pillow slips. A lace-trimmed powder-blue nightie—a spill of finest cotton—lay on the bedcover.

So...under her robe...she'd been naked.

Deliberately deleting the tantalizing image that flowered in his mind, he shucked his linen jacket and tossed it on a chair. With his hands dug into his trouser pockets, he stared out the window.

Darkness had fallen and he could see the halogen lights attached to his warehouses beaming watchful eyes over his car park. He could also see the neon sign above the main entrance doors: Lakeview Construction.

"Quite a view, isn't it!" Kendra's tone was ironic. "Even when you're not here, I can't get away from you!"

He turned.

She'd changed into baggy buttercup yellow sweats that made her look more fragile, more feminine than ever. On her feet were thick white socks with ribbed cuffs; and confining her swooped-up hair was a buttercup-yellow ribbon.

Her cheeks had a pink scrubbed look and she could have passed for seventeen.

"Yesterday's Memories..."

"Why did you come back, Brodie?" She didn't for even a second let her gaze dart to the bed. "If all you wanted to do was say good night, you could have called me."

He picked up one of the glasses and held it out to her. She moved away to draw the curtains, shutting out his sign, shutting out the night. Only then did she take the glass. Holding it by the stem, she dropped into an armchair. Legs curled up under her, she looked up at him warily.

He remained standing; ignored his own glass.

"You and I," he said, "have some unfinished business."

She took a sip of her drink. "This is a very nice wine," she said, ignoring the challenge in his voice and in his words. "French?"

"We need to talk about your making your home here, in Lakeview—"

"I usually buy B.C. wine." She spoke mechanically, as if she hadn't even heard him talk. "It's gaining quite a reputation abroad, you know. Can compete with the—"

"—because if that's what's going to happen, then our two girls will probably become very close. My whole family will be seeing a lot of Megan. I think it would be best if I knew something of Megan's background—"

Finally he'd gotten to her. He saw sparks of amber flare in her eyes.

"For what purpose?" The flame in her eyes was at distinct odds with the chill in her voice.

"For the purpose," he said, "of understanding her. Has she had a happy childhood so far? Was she devastated by her father's death? Jodi was only two when Jack and Maureen were killed—she was lost for the first while, wandered around looking for them...and for her grandpops, but she was young enough that she soon got over—"

"Megan doesn't remember her father." There was a new whiteness around her mouth. "He wasn't around much. Megan and I were very close so losing him didn't affect her as much as it might have. She has no memory of him at all."

"But she is very much a part of him. Fifty percent—isn't that what they say? Children get an equal number of genes from each parent? What kind of a man was he, Kendra? I see a lot of you in Megan, and it's all good. What is there of her father?'' He quirked a questioning eyebrow.

She drank a long swallow of her wine, and then another. And then she drained the glass. She leaned over and set it on a side table.

She rose to her feet.

''You're out of line, Brodie.'' Anger pulsed from her in waves. ''Do you psychoanalyze every child Jodi plays with? If you do...fine! Just don't try to analyze mine!''

But he wasn't going to let her get away with that.

''What's the big secret, Kendra?''

''There *is* no sec—''

''Dammit!'' he shouted, ''don't lie to me! Not again! Why won't you talk about him? What the hell are you hiding? Did the man beat you up? Did he hurt Megan? Tell me!'' He closed the space between them and grabbed her shoulders. ''Tell me *something* about your husband, for God's sake...or I'll start to believe you never had one!''

Her face turned whiter than a snowdrop petal. And her eyes filled with dismay.

In the air was the scent of fear.

Her fear.

''Kendra?'' He felt a clammy chill creep over his skin. ''Is that it? The guy got you pregnant and...then walked?''

She didn't need to speak the answer. It was in her eyes; he could see her shame. Her anguish.

''Dear God.'' Shock had him reeling. It had all been a lie—she'd been living a lie. But why? In this day and age no woman needed to invent a husband;

having a child out of wedlock was no big deal. Questions scrambled around inside him, fighting for answers...but he knew those answers would have to wait. This was not the time to probe.

It was a time to comfort.

With a groan he pulled her close. And as he remembered other occasions when he'd relentlessly tried to delve into her past, remorse spilled through him like dark rain.

Huskily, he murmured apologies, apologies for having pressed her, and distressed her. He was hardly aware that he was running his hands up and down her back; only vaguely aware that her flesh was alive and warm under his fingers through the soft cotton of her sweatshirt.

"So," he said at last, "a make-believe marriage."

"Yes." The word came out grittily. "And a make-believe husband. Megan's father wasn't into commitment—as far as he was concerned, I was a one-night stand. He didn't even hang around long enough to find out if I was pregnant."

"So...you never told him?"

"No." Her voice was muffled against his chest. "I decided both Megan and I were better off without him..."

He tilted up her face. And framed her tear-stained cheeks in his hands.

She was beautiful. And she was irresistible.

He could no more have stopped from kissing her than he could have stopped the sun from rising. But as he lowered his head, it came to him suddenly that his plan was on the brink of fruition—his plan to make love to her, and this time be the one to walk away. He'd formulated that plan, however, before he knew she'd been hurt in the past. No way could he go through with it now; no way could he love her and leave her…as that other man had done…

Then his mouth was on hers and all sensible thought scattered from his head. Her lips were sweet as the nut-pear wine; her skin as smooth as a sun-warmed grape. The gardenia bath perfume that had drifted to him earlier was now intermingled with the pheromones exuded by her heated flesh. An intimate sultry scent that lay between musk and magic.

Moments ago, he'd been drowning in a river of tenderness. Now lust catapulted him out of calm waters and into a savage storm of desire.

He unraveled the yellow ribbon confining her up-swept topknot, letting her long hair fall over his knuckles like gossamer. With an in-hissed breath, he ran his hands through the glossy strands again and again; drawing her hair down over her back; caressing it to the still-wet tips…trespassing beyond them to the dip of her waist…

To the tempting pout of her behind.

She whimpered. A low sound, deep in her throat. With a growl, he cupped her bottom and hauled her close. And as the jut of his arousal pressed into her belly, her whimper caught on a choked gasp.

At the sound, adrenaline surged through him; he'd never felt more powerful…nor more arrogantly, aggressively male.

He slipped urgent hands under her sweatshirt, felt the faint outline of her ribs under his fingertips. He pushed up the sweatshirt, ran his palms around to her breasts. The crests were already taut, quivering, expectant. Excitement roared in his ears, the rush of blood almost deafening him.

So intent was he on having her, he didn't realize she was pushing him away, not until she wrenched herself free with a protesting cry. "No!" She stumbled backward, her eyes wild with panic. "No, Brodie! I don't want to..."

He was panting. It was a harsh sound in the utter stillness of the room. Harsh and ragged. Uncontrolled.

Goddammit! He wanted to rant and roar and—

"I'm sorry." She'd tugged down her sweatshirt, and now wrapped her arms around herself. Her cheeks were flushed bright pink, her eyes had a feverish glitter. "I shouldn't have let you—come in. This is...it'd never work, Brodie. So let's not start something we can't finish."

"Why couldn't it work?" he demanded. "You think I'm like that other guy?"

"No, of course not!"

"Then...*what?* What's holding you back?"

Her eyes clouded over. "I...don't want to talk about it."

He looked at her for a long moment and then his upper lip curled in disgust.

"What a copout!" He grabbed up his jacket and slung it savagely over his shoulder. "At least have the guts to say what's on your mind! You're a Westmore, and I'm a Spencer, and never the twain shall meet. You really haven't changed one bit, have you! Oh, you're maybe eight years older than you were when you left Lakeview, but at heart you're still the same arrant snob you were then!"

He spun on his heel and strode toward the door.

"Brodie, you're wrong—"

"Like hell I am!" He snatched the door open. But just before he charged out, he turned briefly. "I don't want to make the same mistake I made earlier,'' he rasped. ''Good night, Ms. Westmore. Good night... and goodbye!''

Kendra slumped down in the nearest chair.

Why had she surrendered to his kiss? Why hadn't she pushed him away immediately...instead of melting in his arms and giving in to the fever drumming through her veins?

She looked at the yellow ribbon, lying discarded on the tufted beige carpet. Her lips downturned in a bitter smile. Brodie wanted a relationship, he'd made that clear when he'd demanded to know why ''it wouldn't work'' between them.

But if she ever told him the truth about Megan, he'd surely discard her, too, just as swiftly as he'd discarded her ribbon. He'd never marry her, not after he found out the truth about Megan. He'd find it repellent to bring a child into his family when the father of that child was unknown. He'd already made it clear he wanted to know more about Megan's background, because of her growing friendship with Jodi. And she couldn't fault him for that. Responsible parents kept close tabs on their children's friends.

She got to her feet and walked over to the window. Tugging back a corner of the curtain, she looked out into the night.

Lakeview Construction stared right back at her.

She'd spoken the truth, earlier, when she'd told Brodie that even when he wasn't with her, she couldn't get away from him...

She let the curtain drop, and walked back across the room to pick up the yellow ribbon.

He was still with her now, even with the curtains

closed, and not because she'd closed out his sign. He was still with her because he had found a place in her heart.

A very special place.

And one that he would hold forevermore.

Brodie punched his pillow savagely and with a restless mutter heaved himself around onto his back. Elbows bent, he gripped the bedhead's iron frame and glowered up at the ceiling, its stark white dappled with shadows cast by the moonlight and the leaves of the giant oak tree in the yard.

For more than eight years, he had managed to block it out of his mind…the day of the Black Bats concert in Seattle. But tonight, with her sweet body in his arms again, with her sweet will so close to surrender, it had all come tumbling back again.

And like the contents of Pandora's Box, there was no shoving those memories back whence they came; once set free, they took on a life of their own.

He groaned, as they teased and taunted him, dragging him back to a time he had hidden—he'd hoped for good—in the very farthest reaches of his mind…

With three of his co-workers, he'd driven down to Merivale Park, leaving Lakeview at dawn, in a rusty beat-up old van. One of them—Dirk Grayson?—had won four tickets to the concert; they'd been looking forward to it for weeks.

The West Coast had been languishing in an Indian Summer. The weather that day had been scorchingly hot; the beer in their cooler ice-cold. And excited anticipation had buzzed through the enormous crowd in Merivale Park like a swarm of honey-hungry bees.

Man, life couldn't have been better!

He remembered thinking that as he'd lined up at one of the concession stands. He'd already shucked his shirt, and with the sun on his bare back, the aroma of grilled burgers and fried onions in the air, and crisp bills crackling in his wallet...yeah, this was shaping up to be a perfect day!

He'd been grinning as he made his way from the stand.

And then someone had jostled by him, some blond who hadn't been looking where she was going, and she'd knocked the burger from his hand before he'd even taken one bite!

"Hey!" he'd protested. "Look what you've—"

He'd done a double take. Like never before. Was he seeing things? It couldn't be...could it?

She was staring up at him, and she seemed just as shocked as he was.

"I'm sorry!" Kendra Westmore's voice shook. And her big brown eyes, he noticed, were dark with anxiety. Dark as walnuts. "I wasn't looking where I was going..."

The crowd was milling around them and Brodie guessed his burger was now squashed flat under somebody's foot. Not that he gave a damn, because that same crowd was also squashing him against the girl of his dreams. He felt dizzy as he smelled the wildflower scent of her hair and the smell of the coconut oil sheening her bare shoulders.

"Let me buy you another," she said, pushing back a little to unzip her canvas shoulder bag.

It was pastel pink; the same color as her tank top. Her shorts were white, and a pink-and-white checked ribbon confined her hair in a ponytail. The sun's rays whispered in and out of the silken strands, one minute gold, the next platinum, the next straw-yellow. He stared, mesmerized. He'd never been this close to her before; had never realized her hair held so many shades of blond.

She cleared her throat. "I'll buy you another."

He swallowed to relieve the sudden dryness of his mouth. "Oh...no, that's OK." He looked around at the thousands of people crammed together in the park—eating, drinking, talking, laughing. "Who're you here with?"

She didn't answer.

He turned and looked down at her. Her cheeks were pale, her lips trembled. He raised his eyebrows.

"I was with my cousin," she said in a low voice. "Ashleigh. She's nineteen—lives in Seattle. Anyway...she bumped into somebody—some man she'd known before—he wanted her to go with him." Her shoulders lifted in a helpless shrug. "She went."

Brodie felt a snap of anger. "She deserted you?" God, the girl looked terrified; and no wonder! Once darkness fell, this would be no place for a teenager on her own—especially one who looked like Kendra Westmore!

"I'm to meet up with her after the concert, at her car." She swiveled round and gestured toward an enormous willow tree on the western edge of the park. "She's parked over there." Her hand came up to smooth back a wisp of hair from her brow. "Look, I'm sorry about your burger. But if you really don't want another one, then...I'll let you go."

Let him go? *Let him go?* He almost laughed aloud. He'd been obsessed with this girl for almost as long as he could remember; was he going to pass up this chance? Yeah, if you believe that, I have a bridge I'd like to sell you!

"You can come and sit with us." He tried to sound casual, as if he didn't give a hoot whether she came or not. "I'm with three guys I work with at Lakeview Construction. We came down here early this morning in a van."

He saw the look of hesitation on her face, and he felt a sinking feeling in his gut. She'd never spoken one word to him before today. She was the Westmore princess; he was the guy from the wrong side of the tracks. The guy whose old man worked in the Westmore gardens.

"No," he said. And there was a trace of bitterness in his tone despite his effort to keep it out. "I guess you'd rather spend your time alone than with Brodie Spencer!"

A flush of color had seeped over her pale cheeks. She looked up at him steadily.

"No," she said, and for the very first time, she smiled at him. "Thanks, I'd like that."

They spent the rest of the day hanging out with the guys. Then as soon as it got dark, Dirk brought the beer from the van.

At first, she'd been reluctant to try it. In the end, she'd taken a sip from his can. And in the moonlight, he'd seen the widening of her eyes.

"It's good," she said. "I've never tasted it before."

"Here, have a can to yourself..."

She'd smiled. "No, thanks. I'd rather have a pop."

So he'd given her a pop.

And while he'd finished his beer, he hadn't drunk another till the final intermission. He'd been content to lie back on the grass and look at her as she sat beside him, arms looped around her knees, her gaze fixed raptly on the performers on stage...except when, occasionally, she peeked down at him with a shy smile.

When the intermission was almost over, while everybody was waiting for the Bats to come on stage, he sat up, put his arm round her, and whispered in her ear,

"Would you like to split with me, see if we can find a quiet spot, listen to the rest of the concert on our own?"

He'd heard her breath catch. And even in the shadowy dark had seen the flare of something in her eyes; the same flame that was burning him up with a restless fever.

"Yes," she whispered back. "Let's split."

They had found a deserted spot, way back from the fringe of the crowd. He'd taken his shirt with him, and he'd spread it out on the warm grass, under a young willow tree whose leafy branches arced around them in fronds, letting the moonlight dance over them as they kissed.

The passion that had exploded between them was like nothing he could ever have imagined; and the shattering discovery that she had given him her virginity had brought him close to tears.

That night, before they parted, she'd promised that from then on, she'd be Brodie Spencer's girl.

And she'd promised to phone him next day, as soon as she got back to her residence at U.B.C.

He'd watched her slip through the crowd to join her cousin; watched till he saw the car—a Probe—exit out onto the road.

Then feeling happier than he ever had in his life, desperately looking forward to hearing from her again, he'd gone back to join his buddies.

Now, as the memories pressed in on him, torturing him, he felt the old anger swell up in him again. She'd never phoned. And when he'd eventually managed to track down her number and call her, she hadn't picked up the phone. For eight days straight, he called. Before giving up.

He realized he'd been a fool. Realised that in the harsh light of day, she'd wished she'd never even met him. And he vowed not to think about her again.

Three months later he heard she'd come home to Lakeview for Christmas. He made no attempt to contact her.

And then—on Christmas Eve, he'd bumped into her outside the medical clinic. Literally bumped into her. She hadn't been looking where she was going. He'd grabbed her to steady her, and she'd looked so beautiful in a powder blue ski jacket, with her blond hair a ripple of white gold, her skin pale as milk, he'd forgotten all the promises he'd made to himself.

"Kendra!" He'd tightened his grip urgently. "I want to *talk* to you!"

She'd stared right through him as if she didn't even know he was there. Her eyes, those beautiful luminous brown eyes, were dead. She'd made him feel like—

He'd dropped her like a hot potato.

And as he watched her take off along the street at a run—as if she couldn't get herself far enough from him, fast enough—he swore he'd never again try to talk to her about what had happened between them. He'd *never* demean himself that way again!

And when she'd come back to town last week, he'd renewed his vow.

He was pretty damned sure *she'd* never bring up the subject—but he was determined on one thing: *he* certainly wouldn't! She'd already denied him twice: the first time, by not phoning him as she'd promised; and the second, by rejecting him that Christmas Eve.

And then...last night...she'd denied him again.

I've never tasted beer before, she'd said in a butter-wouldn't-melt-in-her-mouth voice.

Never? he'd insisted.

Never, she'd retorted.

And she'd laughed. A cool laugh, calculated to dismiss every single thing that had ever been between them—even the beer he'd shared with her that night, the first beer she'd ever tasted...or so she said.

But how could he believe her anymore?

Deep in his soul, he'd always understood why she'd rejected him: having sex with Brodie Spencer had been a mistake and one she had no intention of repeating.

But he had never figured her for a liar.

And how wrong he'd been about that!

Kendra drove around to the Spencer place next morning at nine to pick up Megan.

Hayley came to the door. "Megan's ready," she said. "Would you like to come in for a coffee?"

"I've had my quota for the morning," Kendra said with a smile. "But thanks anyway—and thanks for baby-sitting."

"After the way you pitched in this past week, I owe you more than *one* night of baby-sitting. Next time you and Brodie want to go out, just give me a call."

There won't be a next time, Kendra reflected bleakly. Brodie had made that quite clear. With one word, he'd said it all. *Goodbye!* "Thanks, Hayley, I'll bear that in mind. Could you send Megan out? I'll wait for her in the car."

What a coward she was—afraid that Brodie might appear, and lance her again with those angry hostile eyes.

She returned to the car and a few moments later, Megan ran out, beaming as she skipped across the lawn. Before strapping herself into her seat, she scrambled over the gearshift and gave her mother a big hug. Then as the car drew away, she waved to Jodi who was standing in the doorway.

Brodie was nowhere to be seen.

Thank goodness for small mercies...

"Mr. Spencer is really grouchy today," Megan said as they drove down the street. "Jodi said he must be getting sick or something 'cos he's never grouchy. No matter what. Anyway, he always helps with the housecleaning on a Saturday morning, but since you already did most of it, he's taken off somewhere. But he'll be back at lunchtime."

She sounded suddenly subdued, her initial bubbly excitement faded.

"What's wrong, honey?" Kendra threw her a glance.

Megan sighed. "I was hoping Jodi would get to invite me round in the afternoon—"

"You didn't invite yourself, did you?"

"'Course not, Mom! I know that's rude. Anyway, even if I had it wouldn't have been any good. Jodi's dad took her aside before breakfast and she told me after that he'd reminded her that Saturday afternoons had always been strictly for family and she mustn't ask anybody over again.''

Kendra wondered if he had resurrected that rule because of their fight last night. If that was the case, then it was mean-spirited of him to take his resentment of her out on her daughter. Was he that kind of man? She hadn't thought so.

''And that upset you.''

Megan slumped back. ''I'm not family.''

''No,'' Kendra said quietly, ''you're not family.'' Nor ever would be.

She could understand why Megan felt so miserable and she felt overwhelmed by compassion for her. Megan was an only child—perhaps a lonely child—but this past week she'd been accepted into a big warm family and had experienced firsthand the fun and camaraderie of having siblings. She'd had a tantalizing taste of what it would be like to be one of Brodie's bunch...and she hungered for more.

She, Kendra, would naturally try to make up for what her daughter was missing...but how could she hope to compete with what the child had found at the house on Calder Street!

CHAPTER TEN

SEPTEMBER passed, and with it the warm weather. Mornings dawned crisp and cold, the leaves on the maple trees started to turn, and fresh snow appeared on the mountaintops.

Kendra was still in the motel and she was restless; impatient to be home...but even more impatient to be away from the Lakeview Construction sign, whose neon lights seemed to taunt her...

The Monday after their altercation, Brodie had turned the Rosemount project over to a man called Sam Fleet. In the days that followed, Sam advised her on the purchase of new appliances and helped her with the many other decisions that had to be made in the refurbishing of her kitchen.

Of Brodie, she saw nothing.

Megan and Jodi were still best buddies, but they rode their bikes back and forth when they visited each other. Jodi's dad never came near Rosemount...and Kendra was never again invited to the house on Calder Street.

She often caught herself thinking wistfully of the fun she'd had there with Brodie's bunch...but as for Brodie himself, she determinedly blocked him from her mind.

And she pretended only a vague interest when Megan announced one evening, as they sat chatting in their motel unit, that Mr. Spencer was dating Mitzi's sister Fifi.

"That's nice." She picked up the *TV Guide* from the coffee table and set it on her lap. "Have you met her?"

"Oh, yes. She works in the cafeteria at school."

"Oh. Is she...pretty?"

"Actually, she looks just like her." Megan stabbed an index finger on the cover of the *TV Guide.* "That could even be her twin. Yup, she's Fifi's double, all right!"

Kendra gazed at the picture and felt a sinking sensation in the pit of her stomach.

And from that moment on, no matter how hard she tried to convince herself that she cared not a whit that Brodie was dating a Marilyn Monroe lookalike, it just didn't work.

On a frosty Thursday morning toward the end of October Sam Fleet phoned to tell Kendra she could return to Rosemount.

In anticipation of the call Kendra had already packed and after she put the phone down she called the front desk and made arrangements to have someone deliver her boxes. As she put down the phone she glanced across the street and her gaze flicked to the neon sign.

Thank heavens she wouldn't have *that* staring her in the face anymore! She swung up her pink anorak and her purse, and made for the door.

She couldn't wait to get home.

Home to Rosemount...and to new beginnings!

Brodie heard the Honda come skimming up the drive.

He stood in the foyer, his back to the open door, his gaze fixed on the mahogany staircase. His heartbeat had hitched at the sound of the car engine; now as Kendra's light steps crunched over the gravel forecourt, the beat lurched forward. She would have seen his truck, parked out front. He fisted his hands. And waited.

She was off the gravel now, running up the steps.

Coming through the doorway.

He sensed the exact moment she saw him.

And stillness fell over the house.

But just for three seconds.

"What are *you* doing here?" Her voice was taut.

He took in a deep breath and turned. His heartbeat staggered like a drunken man. Jeez, he'd forgotten how gorgeous she was! Her hair hung straight like a sheet of white gold, her eyes were dark as bitter chocolate, her skin as smooth as cream.

"I came up to inspect the kitchen," he said. "I always do a final inspection, before I sign a project off."

"So...have you done it? That final inspection?"

"I'm all through with that. Sam's done a fine job."

"So...why are you still here?"

"We can get you that staircase you were so set on...if you still want it, that is. I had to check with you—"

"You could have phoned. But yes, I still want it."

"I can't persuade you to change your mind?"

"No."

She was one stubborn witch. "Your grandfather would turn in his grave if he knew what you were—"

"Let him turn!" She dropped her purse on the hall table. "If you refuse to tear down the staircase, I'll find some other construction firm to take over from here.''

''We have a contract.''

''*Fine!* But I'm the one calling the shots!''

He sighed. Put his palms up, in surrender. ''You're the boss. Ma'am. But will you tell me one thing? *Why?*''

Her chin lifted in a defiant tilt. ''It's dangerous.''

''In what way, dangerous? The structure's sound, I've checked it—''

''It has nothing to do with the structure. Megan persists in sliding down the banister and I'm afraid she'll fall and hurt herself. Break a leg, her neck—'' She sliced out a hand in a brusque ''need I say more?'' gesture.

''You've told her to keep off it?''

''Of course.''

''And she still—''

''Whenever she thinks I'm not around. We've been up here quite a bit during the past few weeks, and I've caught her several times, shooting down it like a rocket. Once the staircase is gone, the problem will no longer exist.''

''Have you told her what you plan to do?''

''No. I made the decision, I saw no reason to discuss it with her.''

He frowned. ''Look, don't take offense, but... you're going about this the wrong way—''

''She's not your child! You're not the one who's doing the worrying!''

''No, she's not my child, but if she were, I'd handle this differently. Sure, Megan's fearless and daring, and I can see how this long banister would be a nearly irresistible temptation to her, but she's an intelligent kid and if you just explained the ramifications of what—''

He broke off as he heard a crunching sound on the gravel outside, and they both turned toward the doorway.

A moment later, Megan shot into the foyer, calling out, ''Hi, Mom! Where—oh, you're there! Oh, hi, Mr. Spencer!''

''Megan!'' Kendra's expression was anxious. ''What's wrong, honey? Why aren't you in school?''

''I forgot to bring money for Hot Dog Day and you said I could never borrow so the teacher gave me permission to pop over to the motel at recess and get it. The lady at the desk said you were here, so I biked up to look for you.''

Kendra glanced at her watch. ''You're going to be late. Recess will be over by the time you cycle back.'' She scooped her purse from the table, gave Megan a couple of dollars, and said, ''Come, I'll drive you to school.''

''But then I won't have my bike for getting home!''

''How about if I drive you, poppet?'' Brodie offered. ''I'll throw your bike in the back of the truck.''

Megan's face lit up. ''Wow, thanks, Mr. Spencer. I really appreciate it.'' She danced toward the door. ''Can we go now, please, so I don't get in trouble?''

''Sure.'' Brodie started after her.

''Brodie...'' Kendra's voice halted him.

He turned. ''Yeah?''

''About...what we were talking about...?''

''I have appointments for the rest of the day but I'll get back to you on it and we'll talk again. OK?''

''All right,'' she said.

But her features had a determined set, and he knew

that unless he came up with some way to stop her, Rosemount's antique mahogany staircase would soon be history.

When Megan came home from school that afternoon, Kendra met her in the foyer.

"Hi, honey," she said. "Did you get back to school in time this morning?"

"Yes, Mr. Spencer got me there just as the bell was ringing." Megan dropped her backpack on the Persian rug. "Mom." Her tone was earnest. "You mustn't get rid of the staircase. I promise, cross my heart, I'll never *ever* slide down it again."

Kendra blinked in surprise. "What on earth made you think of—oh, Mr. Spencer. Did he talk to you about it?"

"Yes, on the drive to school. I'm sorry, Mom, that I made you worried."

"But you already knew I was worried! I told you that, the first time I asked you not to do it!"

Megan pulled a face and looked guilty. "I know."

"So...why the fervent promise now?"

"Don't you believe me?"

"Yes, of course I do. You and I know we can always count on each other's promises! But...I don't understand what Mr. Spencer could have said to persuade you to—"

"Oh, that." Megan's gaze drifted to the staircase. "He said we'd need it, for when Prince Charming comes."

"Prince Charming?"

"Mmm. Mr. Spencer said that one day you would meet your Prince Charming. And he said Rosemount was a perfect house for a wedding, and the staircase was especially perfect, for the most beautiful princess in the world—that's you—coming down, with all your guests watching, to marry your Prince Charming. And it would just not be the same with a modern wrought-iron staircase. Is there any pop in the fridge?"

"Oh..." Kendra swallowed, hard. "Yes, I... brought up some ginger ale and orangeade."

Megan skipped away along the corridor.

Leaving her mother staring unhappily at the magnificent staircase. She'd felt her throat tighten as she'd listened to Megan repeating Brodie's words... especially the part about one day meeting her Prince Charming.

Brodie Spencer was the only Prince Charming she'd ever wanted. But he had no idea she was in love with him!

Heart aching, she clasped her hands around the newel cap and for one yearning moment allowed herself to dream. To picture herself as a radiant bride shyly descending the blue-carpeted staircase to wed the man she adored...

She sighed, and brushed away a tear. It would never happen. She was afraid to tell Brodie the truth; afraid it would change the way he looked at her...and at Megan.

Megan. Now if *she* knew the truth, with all its implications, she'd still go right to Brodie and tell him. She'd take the risk...and damn the consequences.

How she wished she had her daughter's courage.

As she was walking to the kitchen, she heard the phone ring.

By the time she got there, Megan had picked it up.

"It's for me, Mom," she said. "It's Jodi."

Kendra nodded absently and took a can of ginger ale from the fridge. Popping it open, she sipped from it and let her gaze wander around the new kitchen.

Lakeview Construction had done a wonderful job...and Sam Fleet's input re color and design had been invaluable. Although the new cupboards and appliances were starkly modern, the color scheme of white and taupe with touches of red, along with the strawberry motif used throughout, gave the kitchen a warm and cozy look. A look she loved...

"Mom." Megan put her hand over the mouthpiece. "Hayley's going to cook a gynormous lasagne tomorrow night, for a birthday dinner for me, and then I'm invited to sleep over. She says it's 'cos it's my birthday tomorrow and she knows we haven't organized a party yet since we weren't really sure when we'd get back into the house. Is that OK?"

Kendra felt weighed down by guilt. Tomorrow wasn't *really* Megan's birthday—her birthday had been in July...but it had passed unacknowledged, except in Kendra's heart.

"Of course," she said. "And thank Jodi. What time?"

Megan took her hand from the mouthpiece and said eagerly, "My Mom says yes thank you Jodi...and what time?" Her eyes gleamed. "OK. See you at school tomorrow then—"

"Megan." Kendra crossed the kitchen. "I'd like to speak to Hayley if she's around."

"Is Hayley there? My mom wants to speak to her." A pause, then Megan held out the receiver. "Here, Mom."

Kendra took the phone. "Hayley? It's kind of you

to have a party for Megan. I was planning to bake a birthday cake for tomorrow's dinner…I'd still like to do that, and I'll bring it down…"

"Thanks, that'd be great," Hayley said. "Could you make a really big one? There'll be a whole bunch of us—Zoe's coming, and Jack has invited his buddy…"

After she hung up, Kendra said to Megan, "What time do you have to be there?"

"Jodi said we have to be there at six."

"We?"

"Well, you, too, Mom. I thought you knew. They invited both of us and I said yes for both of us. As if they would invite me for a birthday dinner and leave you alone!" She shook her head in disbelief. "You should know the Spencer family would never do *anything* like that!"

Kendra gazed back, feeling the same disbelief Megan was obviously feeling, but for a different reason.

And her heartbeat was fluttering wildly like the wings of a captured sparrow. Would Brodie be at the party?

And if so—perish the thought—would Fifi be there, too?

At exactly six o'clock, Kendra rang the front doorbell of the Spencer residence, and Hayley ushered her guests in.

After taking their jackets, she led them across the cluttered hall toward the closed door of the sitting room.

"Jodi's in here," she said casually. And opening

the door, she stepped back and pushed Megan forward.

"Surprise!" shrilled a chorus of eager young voices.

Kendra's mouth fell open as she looked over Megan's head and saw more than a dozen little girls jumping up and down and shrieking with excitement.

Zoe was perched on the arm of a chair.

Brodie was behind the bar.

And he was alone.

Their eyes met, and she saw his eyebrows rise. As if he was surprised to see her.

Cheeks flushing, she dragged her gaze away.

Jodi had scooted over and was dragging a dazed and dazzled Megan over to the group of children.

"You have to open all your presents before dinner!" Jodi announced. "Here." She thrust a gaily wrapped parcel at Megan. "Start with mine!"

They all clustered around Megan as she sat on the rug and started ripping open Jodi's parcel.

"I invited all the girls in the class," Hayley said to Kendra as Zoe ambled over. "Will you excuse Zoe and me now? We need to set up the table in the kitchen."

They left, and Kendra could see no option but to join Brodie. She forced her legs to take her to the bar. Forced herself to climb onto one of the bar stools. She set her bag on the counter and twined her hands together on her lap.

"Whose idea was this?" she asked. He was looking mouth-wateringly gorgeous in a sapphire polo shirt and silver-gray slacks.

"Hayley's," he said.

"You...didn't have to...be here," she said.

"Surely you have more exciting things to do on a Friday evening than come to a kids' party."

"Like what?"

She shrugged. "Like take somebody out."

"Somebody?"

"Some...woman." Bite your tongue! she told herself in dismay. But her voice seemed to have a mind of its own. "I heard you were dating...your office manager's sister."

"Fifi? Yeah, I've been taking her out...but not dating per se. We've been friends for years. Her husband just walked out on her, she needed a shoulder to cry on." His gaze was steady. "I'm a good listener. Anybody's got problems...worries...secrets to spill, I'm their man."

She almost flinched from his direct gaze. She had the disturbing feeling that he knew she had a secret and was trying to delve into her heart and find out what it was.

"Then Fifi's very lucky," she said. "To have found someone she can confide in. Someone she can trust." Before he could respond, she said lightly, "Mmm, that pink punch looks delicious! Could I have a sample, Mr. Bartender?"

His mouth twisted in a faintly cynical smile and she knew he was aware that she'd deliberately changed the subject. But he made no comment on it.

"Raspberry punch coming up," he said, moving over to the glass punch bowl set at the end of the bar. He used a ladle to fill two round glass mugs with the sparkling drink.

He pushed one mug across the bar to her.

"Cheers!" he said, and raised his glass.

Her own, "Good health!" was drowned out as the

children screamed "Ooh!" and "Lucky you!". She turned. Megan was ecstatically holding aloft a mustard-yellow pocket radio.

"From Hayley and Zoe!" she cried. Then on to the next present with the noise becoming even more deafening.

"I have to thank you—" Kendra had to raise her voice over the babel "—for talking to Megan about the staircase. You were right. I was taking the wrong approach. I totally overreacted—"

"You love Megan and you wanted to protect her. There's nothing wrong with that...to an extent...but at some point, you have to hand her some responsibility for her own safety. Otherwise, she'll never learn."

"Yes, I know. It's just...well, it's hard, because she's all I've got in the world."

"That's your choice."

"Yes," she said. "That is my choice."

He frowned. "Megan's eight, eight years old today. Has there been...nobody...in your life, since..."

She shook her head.

"Once burned," he murmured. "Was that it?"

"Something like that."

"Fifi's been burned, but she's not going to let one bad experience sour the rest of her life. She's moved swiftly from her initial shock and hurt to a healthy raging anger. That'll pass, too. Heck, she's only thirty and she knows she's got a lot of life left to live. And she doesn't want to live it alone. She still believes in marriage..."

"You're a fine one to give advice! You're twenty-seven and you're not married or even thinking about marriage—"

He opened his mouth to say something but she drove on. "Granted you've had three children to take care of, and granted that you didn't want to bring a woman into this house...specially for Hayley's sake. But I know Hayley would have no objections now if you were to take a wife—"

"How the heck do you know that?"

Kendra wished she hadn't said what she had, but there was no taking it back. "Don't ask me how I know. Just accept that I do have it on good authority."

Brodie's eyes narrowed. "I've heard Jodi and Megan whispering. Does this have something to do with Hayley going away to college next year?"

Might as well be hung for a sheep as a lamb. "She's not going to go, unless you've found someone."

"Found someone?"

She suppressed a sigh. And squeezed the word out. "Married."

"So...she wants me to take a wife." He drained his glass, set it down. "Does she have any candidates in mind?"

Kendra slid her eyes away, unable to meet his curious gaze. Her cheeks felt as if they were on fire.

Tension snapped into place between them.

"You," he said slowly. "She's set herself up as matchmaker, and this party..." He blew out a frustrated breath. "Now I know why she *insisted* I be here. Now I know why she neglected to mention that you were invited, too. She didn't even let your name pass her lips till just a few moments ago, when the front doorbell went, and she said airily, 'Oh, that'll be Megan and her mom—did I tell you I'd asked her mom, too?' Did you know I was to be here?"

Kendra forced herself to look at him. "I knew there was that chance."

"And you still came?"

"I can't spend the rest of my life avoiding you."

"Why would you want to?"

Resentment flared through her. *"After what you did?"*

"What did I do?"

She gave him a withering look. "Way back when I wanted someone else to take over my renovations you said to forget it—we had a contract, and I was stuck with you! But when I wouldn't have sex with you that night in the motel you had a temper tantrum and walked from the project…just like a spoiled child, not willing to play the game any longer because the other player wouldn't let you change the rules so they'd be in your favor—"

"I'm not into games," he interrupted harshly. "Not where relationships are concerned. That night, in the motel, I was playing for keeps."

Playing for keeps.

He had banged his hands on the countertop, clenched into big tight fists. She stared at them, at the tanned skin, the sprinkling of wiry black hair, the strong fingers…the ivory knuckles spelling out his tension.

What did he mean by "playing for keeps"? Was it possible that he meant…what she thought he meant? Heartbeats aquiver, she slowly raised her head to look at him again…and felt a tremor of trepidation when she saw the savage intensity of his expression.

"I'm talking marriage," he said. "With you, I'm

not interested in anything less. All...or nothing. So...there you have it." His mouth twisted self-derisively. "The no-good Spencer kid wants to marry the Westmore princess. How's that for—"

"Brodie." Her tone was anguished. "I'm no princess. That story you told Megan...about Prince Charming and the staircase...you're so wrong about me. I'm no princess—"

A delighted scream rent the air and Megan shot over to the bar to join them.

"Look, Mom, this is the board game we've been hunting all over for! Oh, thank you, Mr. Spencer!" She ran around the bar and Kendra saw Brodie's Adam's apple jerk up and down...and then she saw him inhale a deep breath and deliberately adjust his intense expression to a smile as he swung Megan up for the hug she wanted to give him.

Setting her down again, he said lightly, "Jodi told me it was on your wish list, poppet, and on your birthday, all your wishes should come true. Now come on over here. Let's get your mark on the wall and next year we'll do it again, see how much you've grown. We've always done that, Hayley and Jack and Jodi have all got their marks here, from their very first birthday."

His voice was strained, but otherwise there was no outward sign of the fierce emotions he'd exhibited to her a moment before. As for herself, she felt shaken to the core. Vaguely she noticed the many pencil markings on the beige wallpaper, but her mind was reeling with what Brodie had just said.

He wanted to marry her.

She was glad she was seated; she was sure that if she stood, her legs would sag and she'd crumple to the floor. Gripping her hands together in her lap, she watched as Brodie stood Megan against the wall, with her back to it, and told her to stretch straight and tall. Then with a pencil from the bar, he marked her height on the wallpaper.

"Now write your name and your birthday date."

Tongue poking out between her lips, Megan carefully did as she was bid.

Just as she was finishing, Jodi ran over. "Come on, Megan, we're going upstairs to set up the Barbies, and we'll play with them after dinner."

"Thanks again, Mr. Spencer," Megan said.

As the two children moved away, Kendra said huskily, "Brodie, you're wrong about me—"

He interrupted her with a cool, "Megan's a good few inches taller than Jodi. And she seems more mature in a lot of ways..."

Kendra felt as chilled as if he'd slapped her. He obviously didn't want to resume their earlier conversation. He wanted to marry her and he wasn't interested in any response from her but a straight "yes" or a straight "no." She couldn't give him a "yes"...but it would break her heart to give him a "no."

"Hard to believe," he added, "that there's only three months between them."

He could have no idea that his idly spoken comment had caused a painful pricking of her conscience. But it had, and at that moment, she had never hated her deception more. She was a fake, and because of her, Megan was living a lie. And the web of deceit was spreading with each new day. If only she wasn't such a terrible coward; if only she had the courage to spill out her shameful secret—

She realized Brodie was talking to her again.

She refocused her thoughts.

"Sorry." She wiped shaky fingertips over her brow and felt the skin damp with perspiration. "I didn't catch—"

"Kendra!" Hayley called from the doorway. "Could you come and show me how you do that twisty thing with the serviettes?" Without waiting for an answer, she took off again.

Kendra looked beseechingly at Brodie. One part of her desperately yearned to stay, to talk some more with him. The other part urged her to flee, before she said things she would in all likelihood deeply regret...

Brodie took the decision out of her hands.

"Go ahead," he said with an abrupt gesture. "I'll tidy up in here."

After the briefest of hesitations, Kendra took her bag, slid off the bar stool, and made her way to the kitchen.

And as she helped Hayley and Zoe with the serviettes, she tried to get into the party spirit, but her conversation with Brodie had left her feeling drained.

She'd known, of course, that he was attracted to her; and he'd talked before about having a "relationship" with her. But he'd never given any indication that he had marriage on his mind—

"Thanks, Kendra." Hayley's voice broke into her tormented thoughts. "The table looks really nice now. And I just heard Jack and his buddy come in—let's call everybody through to eat. It's time to party!"

For the rest of the evening, Kendra was never alone with Brodie, not even for one moment. By accident, or by his design, she didn't know.

She left the party just after ten. Brodie escorted her to the car, but made no attempt to start up a conversation. His attitude to her was painstakingly polite, as if she'd been a near-stranger...and before she'd driven halfway up Calder Street, she was wiping away blinding tears.

Once she got home, she couldn't settle.

She tried to read, tried to watch TV...but couldn't concentrate. She just couldn't get Brodie out of her mind. In the end, she decided to soak in a hot bath and go to bed.

But once in bed, she couldn't sleep.

She twisted and turned. And her mind twisted and turned, keeping her wide awake. She went downstairs, drank a mug of hot milk, and tried again. She still felt wider awake than the owl hooting at her from the nearby woods.

At midnight, she finally gave up. Gave up and gave in. She couldn't go on like this any longer. Couldn't and wouldn't. Brodie had opened his heart to her. He deserved to know what was in her heart, too. She had to tell him her secret. Come what may.

He saw her as a princess.

He'd always seen her as a princess.

Would he still feel that way about her when he found out she'd been living a lie?

Would he still feel that way about her when he found out she didn't know who Megan's father was?

She hugged her arms around herself and hunched over as desolation threatened to overcome her. If he turned away from her, he would break her heart.

But what did she have to lose? she asked herself miserably. She wanted him so badly it hurt...and she couldn't possibly be any more unhappy than she was now!

CHAPTER ELEVEN

KENDRA swung her Honda into Brodie's driveway and pulled to a halt with as little sound as possible.

The front of the house was in darkness.

But if Brodie was still up, she figured, he'd probably be in the family room, which was situated at the back.

She got out of the car, shut the door carefully.

As she stood, hesitating, she heard a faint splash!

Somebody diving into the pool.

Was it Brodie? Her heart lurched.

Running the tip of her tongue over suddenly dry lips, she walked through the picket gate and then felt her way in the dark along the side of the house.

When she turned the corner she saw, in the eerie glow of the pool lights, that two people were swimming. Jack and his buddy. By the time she'd reached the edge of the pool, they'd plunged down and were gliding along the bottom.

She waited till they'd resurfaced and then she called, softly, "Jack!"

The boy raked his hair back from his eyes and did a double take. Then he swam over, grasped the edge of the pool apron and looked up. "Yo, Ms. Westmore, what's wrong?"

"Nothing's wrong," she assured him. "I need to talk to your Dad, though. Do you know if he's still up?"

"He's not here."

Kendra was torn between head-spinning relief and stomach-plunging disappointment. The disappointment won out. She'd screwed her courage to the sticking place; she doubted she'd ever get it there again if she had to wait.

But where would Brodie have gone, at this time of night? She was visited by a vivid image of a Marilyn Monroe clone welcoming him with open arms...

Jack grinned. "All that noise got to him. After you left, he took off, too. He's at the other house."

"The...other house?"

"Yeah, Grandpop's old place. On Savanna."

His escape from bedlam. Kendra remembered Jodi teasing him about it. It seemed aeons ago now.

"Number 19," Jack went on. "There's a big maple tree in the front yard. You can't miss it."

Despite Jack's instructions, she drove right past the house before she realized her mistake.

Parking at the curb, she walked back along the street.

Brodie's truck was in the drive. Beyond it, dimly lit by a street lamp, sat the house. It was a bungalow, shabby and matchbox small, with an attached one-car garage.

The house itself seemed deserted; but from under the garage door peeked a long thin pencil of yellow light.

Her pulse raced. Her heartbeats thumped.

You can do it, she whispered grimly. You *must* do it.

She stopped at the garage door, and inhaled a deep breath that came from the pit of her soul. She could hear the lunatic yowl of a nearby cat; and the distant roar of a big rig rumbling through town. But she heard not a sound from the interior of the garage.

She clenched and unclenched her right hand, clenched it again, and then before she could give in to the overwhelming urge to run, she rapped the metal door with her knuckles.

The tinny noise was startlingly loud. She grimaced, and her heartbeats thudded even harder when she heard steps approach.

She fixed her gaze on the pencil of light under the door...and gulped as with a grating sound the door started to rise.

She saw two big feet, clad in black trainers.

She saw scruffy jeans, faded at the knee, faded at the crotch; saw a leather belt with a pewter buckle; saw a black T-shirt snug and taut around a muscular chest; saw a lean face—

"What the hell are you doing here?"

—and the spark of surprise in Brodie's beautiful blue-green eyes.

She gulped again. "I...need to speak to you."

He looked around. "You're alone?"

She nodded.

He reached out, pulled her inside, and rattled the door down again. Cocooning them in a tidy cement-floored garage, which was dominated by...

A shiny black Harley Davidson motorcycle.

Stunned, Kendra stared at it. "Your bike!" She felt dizzy as memories swirled around her. Why did she so often want to cry around this man? "You...kept it."

He shrugged. "Yeah, I've kept it. I work on it, keep it in tiptop shape, for when I sell it—which I plan to, one of these days. I've just never gotten around to it yet but I will...soon. Yeah, soon...I'm gonna get rid of it..."

And cows will fly! Kendra thought. Who is he trying to convince? This bike had been the love of his life; it'd be like ripping out his heart, to part with it.

"When was the last time you rode it?" she asked.

"I put it away when I took on the kids. It was...part of my past. Besides, I needed a vehicle with room for four. I needed something...safe. This bike was no use..."

He probably didn't even realize he was running his gaze caressingly over the gleaming fuel tank cover as he spoke; over the sparkling headlights; the smooth black saddle...

He cleared his throat. "So...what did you need to talk about so badly that it couldn't wait till morning?" He swept up a clean flannel rag from the bench behind him and wiped a smear of oil from his forearm. Tossing the rag back, he raised his eyebrows, leaned against the bench, folded his arms across his wide chest, and waited.

She wondered if her heart could beat any faster without exploding. "You and I...we were talking...in the family room, before Megan interrupted...we didn't finish..."

He said nothing.

Her cheeks grew warm. "I was telling you... about...I wanted to let you know you're wrong about me, Brodie. About saying I'm...a princess. I'm not. I'm..." She laughed nervously. "I've certainly not behaved like a princess."

Still he said nothing. He was not about to help her on this. She skimmed a panicky glance around the garage and saw, behind him, three wooden steps leading up to a door. The door leading into the house. But there was no escape there. No escape anywhere.

She shifted from one foot to the other. And back again. "I've...something to tell you and...well, I think it'll change everything, how you feel about me—"

"You don't know how I feel about you."

His voice, coming at her unexpectedly, startled her. She blinked. "Sorry...?"

"I said, you don't know how I feel about you."

"Well, no, but—"

"You don't know because you don't want to know." His tone was bitter. "You've never wanted to know."

"Brodie, can I...this isn't easy..."

He looked as if he wanted to say something, but after a long tense moment, he growled, "Go ahead."

"And I don't want you to stop me, or interrupt again...just let me tell you everything in one go."

"Fair enough."

She took in a deep breath, and said, "Nine years ago, I went to a rock concert near Seattle with my cousin Ashleigh. She deserted me just after we got there, but I met somebody. We—he and I—stayed together...all through the concert." She swallowed and made herself go on. "We had sex and—" She stopped short when she saw that Brodie's features had tightened abruptly; the veins at his temples bulged. He opened his mouth but she said in a rush, "You promised!"

She thought he was going to renege on his promise. He looked as if he was absolutely *bursting* to say something. But then in the end, glowering, he just muttered a pungent oath and made a curt—angry?—gesture for her to go on.

Her palms felt slick with sweat. She wiped them down the sides of her jeans as she continued.

"I met up with Ashleigh after the concert. On the way home, we were in a car accident. My cousin was OK, but I wasn't. My hip was injured and eventually I had to stay in hospital for a couple of weeks...but...well, when I woke up in my hospital bed the day after the smash...my memory was gone. I couldn't remember anything of the day before, from the time Ashleigh and I split up, till...I came to."

"You...lost your memory?" Brodie's face was stark with shock.

"The doctors called it post-traumatic amnesia. They said it often happens to crash victims, and sometimes the memory comes back." She smiled wanly. "Mine never has."

Brodie was staring at her as if she'd suddenly sprouted green horns. "You remember *nothing* of that concert?"

"Nothing."

"You...don't remember who you were with?"

"No, it's a complete blank. All I know is...on the way home, I'd apparently gotten as far as telling Ashleigh that after the two of us separated I'd met somebody, and stayed with him all through the concert—when wham! this other car smashed into us and I was knocked out cold."

"Dear God!" Every vestige of color had leached from Brodie's face. "I don't believe it—"

"Believe it," she said. "It happened. I had sex with this person...whoever he was..."

Brodie was shaking his head. She thought—she

couldn't be sure but she was *almost* sure—that there was a shine of tears in his eyes.

Well, she thought with an unaccustomed feeling of cynicism, nobody likes having their fantasies shattered.

And now that she'd shattered his and seen the effect, her own hurt and bitterness drove her to turn the knife.

"He could have been a stranger." Her voice was so harsh she didn't even recognize it. "And may well have been. At that time I didn't have a man in my life and there was no one among my male friends that I would have slept with. Yet on the morning I arrived at that concert, I was a virgin...and when I left to go home, I was not. So you see, Brodie, I'm no princess. A princess would never have behaved the way I did. I gave myself to somebody—somebody I'd possibly never met before that—" Tears almost choked her but she knew she had to go on. "And there's more..."

Brodie pushed himself away from the bench, and walked away from her, toward the steps leading into the house.

Aghast, she stared after him, struggling to overcome a feeling of disbelief. She had, of course, known this might happen. She'd told herself from the very beginning that he might want nothing more to do with her when he found out what she'd done. But somewhere, deep in her heart, she hadn't really believed he was that kind of man.

She'd been wrong.

And she hadn't even told him about the pregnancy yet!

But he didn't want to hear any more.

He'd already heard enough.

With an anguished sob, and tears blurring her eyes, she turned and stumbled toward the garage door behind her.

"Kendra." The tenderness in his tone stopped her as nothing else could have done. "Where are you going?"

She turned, slowly, and even through her veil of tears, she saw he was holding out his hand.

"Come," he said simply.

She couldn't move.

He walked over to her. He took her hand. Hers was cold, trembling. His was big and strong and warm.

"Come inside," he said. "I have something to show you."

Show her? What could he have to show her?

Lost in confusion, sniffing back her tears, she let him lead her to the steps, and up into the house.

He flicked on a light, and as he ushered her along the short narrow passage she just had time to see a shadowy sitting room ahead before he stopped at a closed door.

He looked down at her.

"In here," he said in a soft voice.

He opened the door and switched on the light.

"This used to be my bedroom," he said. "It's just as it was when I left here, six years ago."

Her legs felt wobbly as she walked into the room and looked around. It was a small room, and sparsely furnished, with a single bed, a scarred dresser, a homemade desk...

On one wall was a chrome-framed corkboard; on another were four huge posters—

Posters of...the Black Bats.

Somewhere, in Kendra's bewildered mind, a

thought tumbled forward. Brodie must have liked them, too.

He brought her over to the corkboard.

She sensed him watching her intently as she let her puzzled gaze seek out the items pinned on the beige cork.

There were only three.

A ticket stub from the Merivale Park Black Bats concert.

A pink-and-white checked ribbon.

And a photograph—

Her gaze was drawn back to the ticket stub, but her mind seemed to have gone numb.

So...Brodie had been at that concert, too.

She eased closer. Stared at the ribbon.

Then tentatively, fearfully, as if it had been white-hot, she reached out and touched it. It was of the finest taffeta, slightly faded with age...and she'd worn one exactly like it, to tie back her hair, the day of the Black Bats concert.

As if in a dream, she turned her attention to the last item on the board. The photograph.

And when she saw that the glossy colored picture was of Brodie and herself she thought she must be hallucinating. Her throat tightened so she could hardly breathe.

They were leaning together against a van, with the sun at their back, and Brodie had his arm around her. He was looking down at her with the same irresistible smile that had stolen her heart; and she was looking up at him with an expression of such adoration she almost cried out.

"You don't remember?" Brodie's voice was a velvet caress, sending shivers over every inch of her skin.

"You don't remember that night? That night in the park?"

She felt his fingertips on her chin, felt him turn her face up to his. She could see the tracks of tears on his cheeks. Tears welled up in her own eyes so she could barely see him.

"It...was you?" she whispered, unable to believe, to dare to believe. "It was really you?"

"Oh, yes," he said huskily, drawing her into his arms. "It was indeed. And sweetheart, we didn't have sex. *We made love.* And we made promises. You promised me, that night, that you'd be Brodie Spencer's girl forevermore. Are you still my girl?"

"Oh, Brodie." She felt giddy with joy and wonder. Could this really be happening? Was it possible that her darkest nightmares had become transformed into this wildest-dream-come-true? "I've never been anyone else's girl."

And Megan was Brodie's daughter.

Even in her most far-flung fancies, she had never come up with such an unlikely deliriously wonderful scenario. The bliss of it was almost too much to bear—

"Ah, sweetheart," Brodie murmured as he drew her closer, sipped kisses from her brow. "We're together again, at last..."

"Brodie, there's one more thing I have to tell you—we have to talk—about Megan's father—"

"Later," he whispered into her hair. "Later, my love. I've waited far too long for this..."

And as he claimed her lips in a kiss that made her his forever, she somehow managed to contain her overwhelming impatience to share the truth that would make him even happier, if that were possible, than he already was.

But it would keep.

Besides...shouldn't Megan be told first? Surely the child had the right to be told, before anyone else, who her father was? She'd waited so long to have a real family.

Tomorrow, then, she would tell Megan.

And afterward, she would tell Brodie.

With an ecstatic sigh, she gave herself up to Brodie's tender kisses. Tonight would be theirs, and theirs alone.

"Thanks, Hayley!" Megan shouted through the open window of Brodie's Volvo as she left the Spencer house next morning. "It was the funnest birthday party I've ever had!"

"'Bye, Megan!" Hayley and Jodi waved from the lawn as the car drove away.

When they got to the end of the street, Megan wriggled around in her seat and said, "Mr. Spencer, how come Mom didn't come to pick me up like she told me she was going to?"

"I saw your mom later last night—I was up at Rosemount with her for...um...a while. She asked if I'd drive you back home. She said she had a big surprise for both of us."

"What could it be?"

"Your guess is as good as mine, poppet, but since it gets me out of housecleaning this Saturday morning, I'm not complaining!"

Megan chuckled. "You didn't forget any of my presents, did you?"

"No, they're all in the trunk."

"Did Mom tell you she bought me a computer for my birthday? It's for schoolwork but I can play games on it too. It's so cool, and she's set it up in my bedroom..."

As Megan prattled on, Brodie only half listened.

The sun was shining, it was a crisply cold but glorious day, and all was well with the world. With *his* world.

Man, he thought, *life couldn't be better!*

He smiled as he recalled the last time he'd said that to himself. It had been at the Black Bats concert—just minutes before he'd collided with the girl of his dreams.

Now, nine years later, he could hardly believe his luck. Kendra loved him. She'd always loved him. And she'd told him that, last night, in more ways than one...

He glanced at Megan, who was tucking her earphones on and preparing to listen to her new radio. His heart melted as he saw the concentration on her thin face...but at the same time he felt a twinge of anxiety. Overnight, he'd added another child to his bunch...

Then he grinned, and pressed the accelerator down as he hit the long straight stretch of road leading up to the Rosemount hill. Heck, he'd had years of experience with three. Tacking on a fourth would be a breeze!

Megan started to sing along with whatever music she was hearing. And tapping her toes on the vinyl mat at her feet.

He glanced down. And raised his eyebrows. He'd never noticed before but...Megan Westmore had mighty big feet! Not like her mother, who had dainty slender feet. Poor kid must've taken after her father in this regard, he guessed.

Her father.

As he returned his attention to the road, he felt a dark cloud mar his happiness. Kendra had tried to talk to him last night, about Megan's father, and he'd put her off. But then, after, when he'd been the one to bring up the subject, she'd told him they'd talk about it, for sure, tomorrow.

Now tomorrow was here. What was he going to find out? He only knew what she'd told him weeks ago: the man had deserted her and as a result, she hadn't wanted him to have anything to do with Megan.

But...what if the guy turned up some day, out of the blue, and demanded to share custody? The possibility gave him icy shivers. He'd known Megan for only a few weeks, but she'd wound her way into his heart and found a permanent place there. It was *unthinkable* that some stranger could turn up and try to gain joint custody...

He clenched his jaw. He'd make sure he and Kendra did talk about it today. They had to track the guy down and get him to sign papers renouncing any claim to his daughter.

Brodie's hands twisted around the steering wheel as if he were strangling a poisonous snake. Every man had his price. He'd pay *this* particular one whatever it took.

"So you see, sweetie, Mr. Spencer is your dad. I just didn't know it till last night."

Kendra was sitting on a bench in the gazebo; Megan was standing in front of her. Kendra had held her daughter's hands tightly as she told her story, and Megan had listened, wide-eyed and silent, with the scent of summer's last roses drifting to them on the cool breeze.

Now Kendra waited for Megan's response, but the child didn't speak. She just stood there, frowning, her eyes unfocused. It was obvious to Kendra that Megan was mulling over everything she'd heard, trying to understand it all.

Finally, she spoke.

"Does that mean," she said slowly, "that Jodi is going to be my cousin?"

"Yes, Jodi's your cousin...and Hayley and Jack, too."

"And...we'll all live together?"

"Yes, we'll all live together."

"And I'll be...part of the Spencer family? Truly a part of it?"

Kendra felt her heart break as she saw the expression of tentative hope and growing wonder in Megan's brown eyes.

"Yes, sweetie, you'll be part of the family. And you'll be one of Brodie Spencer's bunch."

"Oh, Mom..." With a sob, Megan launched herself at her mother and twined her skinny arms around Kendra's neck. She pressed her face to Kendra's bosom and whispered in a voice that was ragged with tears. "I love Mr. Spencer already, Mom. I love my dad so much I could burst."

Brodie watched, from the sitting room window, till he saw Megan run from the gazebo. She was tearing toward the house, helter-skelter, as fast as her spindly legs would carry her, her blond hair streaming out behind her like a pale banner.

He spun from the window and got to the front door as she sped across the forecourt. He ran lightly down the steps to meet her.

She flung herself at him and he swung her up in his arms.

"Mom told me," she cried. "She said you're my real dad and we're all going to live together and be happy ever after!"

Real dad? What the...? Why hadn't Kendra told her child the truth, that he was going to be her *adoptive* dad? Surely, after last night, she should know that there must be no more lies, not even half-lies or lies by omission, in their family. He'd sort this out with her...but not while Megan was around.

He gave Megan a big bear hug, and then swung her down again. "We're going to be the happiest family that ever was," he said, crouching down to her level. She was swiping away tears and he grinned as he saw the smudges of dirt on her face. "But tell you what—I've got to talk to your mom now. OK?"

She nodded.

"I've carted all your presents into the hall so why don't you take them all up to your bedroom and play for a while. I'm going to take your mom for a walk in the grounds and after we're finished talking, we'll come and look for you."

"OK!" Her smile was beaming.

He straightened and watched as she flew into the house, but once she'd shut the door behind her, his smile faded.

He turned, and saw Kendra walking toward him, across the lawn.

He went to meet her. They needed to talk.

What he *wanted* to do was pull her into his arms, kiss her, bury his face in that shimmering wheat-gold hair...

But that would have to wait. First of all, they had to talk about Megan's father.

Kendra's step faltered.

Why was Brodie scowling?

Was he put out that she hadn't told him the truth last night? And even more put out that he'd had to hear it from Megan? Well, she'd intended to be the one to tell him, but when she'd told Megan that Mr. Spencer didn't know yet that he was her dad, the child had shot off excitedly before Kendra could stop her.

Oh, she'd opened her mouth to call Megan back, but then had closed it again with a rueful smile. She was being selfish; she'd wanted to be the one to tell Brodie, the one to bring that look of bedazzlement to his face when he found out Megan was his.

But...he knew now...and he was scowling.

"Brodie," she said as they met, "what's wrong?"

He rammed his hands into the hip pockets of his jeans, and looked down at her. He was still scowling.

"We have to talk. About what you told Megan."

"I...don't understand!" The sun was blinding her as she looked up at him. She raised her hand and cupped it over her brow to shadow her eyes. "I thought you'd be...pleased." And that was an understatement. She'd thought he'd be over the moon.

"Let's walk," he said impatiently. He grasped her wrist, pulled her hand from her brow. "Come on."

He walked her well away from the house. Past the gazebo, to the path leading over to the woods.

They were almost there before he spoke again.

"Honey," he said quietly, "you have to tell Megan the truth. Why are you letting her believe I'm her real dad?"

Kendra stopped short. And stared at him. "*What* did you say?"

A nerve throbbed in his cheek. "The story you told her...that she was really mine. I know you only have her happiness in mind...but she's got to know, sooner or later, that I'm not her real father. You've got to stop protecting her, Kendra. And I don't want there to be any more...lies."

Lies? Her stomach muscles wrenched into a hard knot. She swallowed over the agonizing lump in her throat. Dear God, what was this? He was saying he...wasn't...Megan's father? Had last night been a dream? Had her nightmare come back? "You're denying that you're Megan's father?"

His bewilderment was obvious. "Sweetheart, even if I hadn't made sure you were protected that night in the park...if by chance there had been an accident and I'd gotten you pregnant, the baby would've been born in the summer. June, maybe July...but *October?*" His laugh was dry. "Not in a million years."

Megan had omitted to tell him about the birthday switch! "Oh, Brodie..." Kendra felt a surge of relief...and couldn't stop the little giggle that burst out.

He glowered again, even more darkly than before. "I fail to see the joke!"

Her eyes twinkled as she put her arms around his waist and looked up at him. "Brodie, darling idiot, we're talking at cross-purposes! You see, despite your precautions, I *did* get pregnant. And Megan was born in July—"

"October!"

"No," she said softly. "I...faked that."

He blinked. Twice. "You've lost me."

"Let me explain. Brodie, I told you Megan was born in Seattle. And we lived there for the first couple of years after she was born. But before I returned to Vancouver, I faked her ID to make her seem three months younger than she was. Her father had never come back into my life after our 'one-night stand' and I wanted to safeguard my secret in case he ever did. I thought that if I put it out that Megan was born in October, if he ever showed up it'd never even occur to him that she might be his. Which of course is what indeed did happen. If *you'd* known Megan was born in July, you'd probably have guessed weeks ago that—"

"Are you saying," Brodie broke in disbelievingly, "what I think you're saying?"

"Yes, that's what I'm saying."

"Megan's really mine? That sweet little kid is mine?"

"Oh, yes, Brodie." Tears filled her eyes as she saw the shine of tears in his. "She's really yours."

He groaned, and pulled her so hard against his chest he winded her. She felt him tremble, and knew he was unbearably moved by what he'd just found out. For a long long time, they just stood like that, holding each other.

Then he whispered gruffly, "If only I hadn't been so damned proud we could have cleared this all up weeks ago. But I was determined not to be the one to bring up that night in the park. You'd denied me so often!" He grasped her shoulders and held her away from him. "Or at least I thought you had. You promised to phone me that Sunday when you got back to the residence, you didn't, and I called you for eight days straight without your picking up the phone—"

"I was in hospital!"

"And then, way back on that Christmas Eve, when I bumped into you outside the clinic, you ignored me—"

"I'd just found out I was pregnant! I was shattered!"

"And then that thing with the beer, when you said you'd never tasted it before…but you had, at the concert, you sipped from my can and said it was the very first time—"

"Oh, Brodie," she sighed, "I hurt you so much, without even knowing it! I promise, with all my heart, that I'll never hurt you again. I'll be the best wife in the world!"

He was grinning now like a kid let loose in the world's biggest candy store. "So—" he looked down at her teasingly "—the snooty Westmore brat wants to marry—"

"That no-good Spencer kid."

He ran his fingertip over her raspberry-pink lips. The scent of her skin drove him wild. "Well," he drawled, his blue-green eyes warm with laughter, "who'd have thunk it!"

"Who indeed!" She batted her long blond lashes seductively and flirted up at him. "Well, for heaven's sake, what are you waiting for, Brodie? Kiss your bride!"

Normally he wasn't a man who reacted well to bossy women. But heck, this was no normal situation, and this, sure as heck, was no normal woman.

"Yes, ma'am," he said. "Pleased to oblige."

EPILOGUE

EXCERPT from the social page of the June 17 *LAKEVIEW GAZETTE*:

Brodie Daniel Spencer, owner of the prosperous Lakeview Construction Company, was married Saturday to Kendra Jane Westmore, granddaughter of the late Edward Westmore. The wedding took place at the Lakeview United Church on Savanna.

The bride looked beautiful in a misty blue dress; the groom elegant in a midnight blue tux. Flower girls for the ceremony were Megan Spencer, the couple's daughter, and Jodi Spencer, niece of the groom. Jodi's sister Hayley, was maid of honor; her brother Jack was best man. Dr. Ben Jamieson gave the bride away.

A dazzling reception for over two hundred people was held at Rosemount, where the couple will take up residence after their honeymoon.

"I had intended to run my old family home as a B and B," the radiant bride remarked to this reporter. "But I'm going to be far too busy to run a business for the next while—as you know, Brodie and I between us have four children—"

"And we plan on adding *at least* four more to the bunch!" the groom interjected, bringing a rosy blush to his bride's cheeks.

For their going-away outfits, both bride and groom wore black leather. Their choice of transportation was a gleaming Harley-Davidson motorcycle which had apparently been in storage for some years at the groom's former home.

The honeymoon destination was kept secret, but rumor had it that the first stop was to be Seattle's Merivale Park, where the couple were to renew vows they had made to each other, many years ago, at a Black Bats concert.

HARLEQUIN PRESENTS®